The LAST PORTRAIT of the DUCHESS OF ALBA

Francisco Goya, *Volaverunt*, Biblioteca Nacional, Madrid.

The LAST PORTRAIT of the DUCHESS OF ALBA

A NOVEL

Antonio Larreta

Translated by Pamela Carmell

ADLER & ADLER

Published in the United States in 1988 by
Adler & Adler, Publishers, Inc.
4550 Montgomery Avenue
Bethesda, Maryland 20814

First published in Spanish in 1980 under the title
Volavérunt copyright © 1980 Antonio Larreta
English translation copyright © 1988 Adler & Adler,
Publishers, Inc.

All rights reserved. No part of this book may be used or
reproduced in any manner whatsoever without written
permission except in the case of brief quotations
embodied in critical articles and reviews.

Larreta, Antonio, 1922–
The last portrait of the Duchess of Alba.

Translation of: Volavérunt.
1. Goya, Francisco, 1746–1828—Fiction. 2. Alba, María
del Pilar Teresa Cayetana de Silva Alvarez de Toledo,
duquesa de, 1762–1802—Fiction. 3. Godoy, Manuel de,
príncipe de la Paz, 1767–1851—Fiction.
I. Title.
PQ8520.22.A7V613 1988 863 87-11469
ISBN 0-917561-42-2

Printed in the United States of America
First Edition

CONTENTS

FIRST NOTICE

Madrid, Spring 1980

If my mother had not married for money so many times, and at the same time had not been so unconcerned about material wealth except when it took on the ascetic and abstract form of a bank account, this book probably would never have been published. But one of her last requests, on her death bed (when, I must say, her glorious pragmatism did not show any sign of failing), was that one of her sons should go to Paris, supplied with the appropriate keys, open the old house on the rue Neuve des Mathurins, and dispose of all the furniture, decorations, knickknacks, and bagatelles that had been there in the cellar since 1940, surviving an occupation, a war for freedom, General de Gaulle, the student uprising in May of 1968 and real-estate speculation. "What you find there probably won't warrant a gala at Sotheby's," she murmured in a voice that was weak, but with its intellectual energy intact. "Lorenzo's strong point was avarice, and considering what the judge awarded me in the divorce, which was a savage slashing, and the hardships of his last years, he most likely has sold off the few family relics to his exiled friends, but . . . who knows? You might turn up something interesting there." I was the son assigned to go to Paris. This Memoir that I am having published today was—along with Second Empire furniture, third-hand at least; brocades crawling with moths; a small collection of *Prix Goncourt*; and other French curios from those days—my interesting find . . .

After four happy and fruitful marriages, the Second World War already on the horizon, my mother decided two things: to marry a fifth time for love and to pick a small South American country as the safest refuge at that time. There she could enjoy in peace both my father and his fortune. Over the years, both decisions proved to be errors in judgment. My father's love and that little country's safety were deteriorating in a similar fashion. The one tormented her with jealousy, about the past as well; the other deceived her—and ended up betraying her—with a socioeconomic crisis that began insidiously and ended in chaos, violence, and bankruptcy. In the final years of her life, my mother had to call on her last reserves of good humor to face a crazy husband, meager income, and several rebel grandsons. And so, the once-disdained house on rue Neuve des Mathurins, a legacy that in its day had seemed to her nearly a display of avarice, became one of the few treasures she could divide before she died, along with her remaining tiny jewels, some furs, already lackluster and threadbare, her government bonds (from a government in alarming bankruptcy) and, yes, her delightful and still very vivid memories of her golden youth. "Errare humanum est" were her last words. She breathed them with a deep sigh and died. I suppose that error implicates all of us—the country, my father, her sons, her grandchildren—the sad remnant of her last forty years. Poor Mother. I hope my "interesting find" will bring her some final consolation.

Lorenzo de Pita y Evora, Marquis of Peñadolida, was my mother's third husband, I believe. She met him in Biarritz about 1932. She had just become a widow for a second time (from the Englishman who consolidated her fortune). The Marquis was leaving Spain in the footsteps of Alfonso XIII, opting for the relative hardships of exile in France. They were married for no more than two years, but my mother must have made a lasting impression on him; to the plunder of that divorce he added—as if it were nothing—of his own and final volition, the legacy of the house on rue Neuve where they had spent that brief, amorous intermezzo.

I don't know if the Marquis found the manuscripts that make up this book in the same disorder that I did and then added them to his own papers, if he found them somewhere else, or if they were sent to him by someone else. He doesn't make that clear in his prologue. It's only my compulsive habit of leafing through old magazines that led me to my second discovery to which without a doubt the first discovery's value corresponds. Some absentminded servant or the lawyer's clerk could have been straightening up the house a little when the Marquis died, someone who did not discriminate between files of paid and unpaid bills, stacks and stacks of *L'Illustration* and *Blanco y Negro,* and this extraordinary document, which the Marquis never managed to bring to light. There I found it, damp, yellowed, ignored, like a cataleptic who has awakened in his tomb and now, worn out and powerless, is unable to declare that he is alive and that someone should revive him from his secure oblivion.

When I learned about the contents of the document and figured out its value, I traveled to Spain to start an investigation into the matter, to corroborate the authenticity of those original documents, to confirm its assertions in other sources, with other testimonies. I have to say that the trip was disheartening. I ran up against suspicion from historians and hostility from government institutions, propelled in the shadows, as I saw it, by class interests, familiar hypocrisies and even vague political forces. And this, forty years after the Marquis had bumped up against the same rocks . . . I stopped my investigations. I documented what I could (my predecessor had already done a lot along this line) and decided finally to have it published, adding my own notes and related material to the Marquis's previous and more extensive ones. So his and my comments appear together throughout the book, except with some obligatory, rare exceptions, which I cite.

Now I yield the floor to the Marquis. What I have called "Second Notice" is, of course, chronologically, the first, although it ends up being second, if we take into account the one by Manuel Godoy which opens the Memoir. One can't help thinking about Russian dolls.

SECOND NOTICE

Paris, April 1939

I HAVE thought a long time before deciding to bring to light this unpublished Memoir of singular historical interest. It fell into my hands through misfortunes gleaned from exile and curiosity one melancholy Paris afternoon in 1937. I was not able to put off reading it until a new day lightened the sky. For many hours, its contents—anxious, astonishing, overwhelming, reiterated—took me back in space to my Madrid, resigned without resignation; and in time, to a past not so remote that there remained no trace of that color and blood, shadows vibrating with crime and pain.

This Memoir returns like a ghost to reclaim justice—but who is the ghost? Who is the victim finally in this story of just one crime but many suspects? This Memoir implicates a group of people, who range from the loftiest grandeur and from posthumous glory to those with the most obscure or insignificant destinies, who belong to a period in the history of Spain and Madrid that spanned two centuries: the happy and carefree end of the eighteenth century and the tragic dawn of the nineteenth, that critical time captured and immortalized by no one better than Don Francisco de Goya y Lucientes. Accordingly, he is one of the people who figure prominently in this *petite histoire.*

The event around which this entire document revolves occurred on July 23, 1802, and was the death of María del Pilar Teresa Cayetana de Silva y Álvarez de

Toledo, thirteenth Duchess of Alba (or Alva, as many historians would have it . . .). Except for a brief police report made a few days after that death, neither the Memoir nor the letters included in it are contemporary with the Duchess's dramatic demise. This story, curiously, was lived by the young and told by the old, more than twenty, nearly fifty years later. This manuscript came to me in French, penned in a hand that does not match that of the person who claims to be the author. I therefore presume this to be a translation of the original text commissioned by its author himself, a fact that leaves room for real doubts concerning its authenticity from the outset.

The work that I have undertaken—that of retranslating this Memoir written so long ago into Spanish—confers on me, I realize, a greater authority (which I declare with no presumptuousness) and allows me to grasp the intimate and almost amorous nature of a piece of literature whose style reveals to us its most subtle and evasive reflections, in the same way we would portray the woman we love. With this authority, I shall venture two definite conclusions: First, that the French text, which has had an affect on me since that autumnal and troubled afternoon, is without a doubt a translation from a Spanish text, originally written in a somewhat flowery, sinuous and solemn style, in a Spain that wavered between the Baroque tradition and the classicist Enlightenment; second, that its author is certainly Don Manuel Godoy, as is stated in the text, and this assertion springs (a) from the comparison with his other writings; (b) from the place where the document was found eighty-six years after his death; (c) from the verification I have managed to gather of many events and vicissitudes narrated in it, verification which, it pains me to say, would have been more complete if I could have conducted it in my own country, and above all, if I could have found more cooperation and fewer prejudices in social and scientific channels, so that I might have proved or refuted those distant facts. I am referring equally to the aristocratic class of Spanish society—or at least to the families historically tied to the facts—and to the institutions of historical investigation.

But Spain continues to be Spain, from afar or close up. Still in the distance is the day when, as Godoy himself says in a passage in his Memoir, it will become a nation "synchronized with the clock of enlightened and modern history."

THE BRIEF AND SECRET MEMOIR OF DON MANUEL DE GODOY, DUKE OF ALCUDIA, written in 1848, concerning the death of María del Pilar Teresa Cayetana de Silva y Álvarez de Toledo, Duchess of Alba, which occurred forty-six years before; the strange circumstances that surrounded that death; and its more veracious interpretation, including the testimony of Don Francisco de Goya and the posthumous letter from another highly placed person indirectly involved in the events, which throws new light on those events.

NOTICE TO THE READER

THE SIX years since the last volume of my Memoirs was published ended a few days ago.[1] Although its title would suggest it to be so, this Brief Memoir should not in any way be understood to be an aside or an appendix to that longer memoir, or as work left over from that project, but rather as a totally independent work, destined to address a very different purpose and written in a contented state of mind, different from that which informed those former memoirs . . .

Which were conceived, written down, and published to the end of justifying for centuries to come the political measures taken by my august sovereigns Their Majesties, the King of Spain, Carlos IV, and his consort, Queen María Luisa, and to humble their vile detractors before the mirror of Truth, requiring that mirror (as my honor and my good name defiled by those same enemies require it) for the restoration of my own rights and power as governor and of the influence that my person and my works had upon the history of the Spanish state during the years of my ministry and until my fall.[2]

This work, which I entitle Brief Memoir, on the other hand, is nothing more than my personal testimony, held back until now from the public, concerning an incident of a private nature to which I was not only witness, but also, in some sense, judge and party: the death of the Duchess of Alba, occurring on July 23, 1802. You may ask me, and I will not be able to answer, why I waited more than forty years before writing this. I will answer my future interlocutor thusly: So often did I hesitate to set this down that, for a long time, I thought I would die with my lips sealed against the clues I had kept secret. On one hand, my arrival at the threshold of my eightieth year and, on the other hand, a moral imperative that some would consider delinquent have been the motives that have finally brought me to publish these memoirs. And now, being very careful to take the precautions that prudence advises, I make these memoirs public with fewer scruples for the very reason that a half century has passed since that unhappy event and the majority of the people who figure in that event in one way or another have passed away,[3] and moreover, I believe myself at this advanced age to be the only person living who can still offer a detailed and truthful chronicle of the event, with no spirit of scandal, calumny, or collaboration with anyone else's story since that would not be in accordance with my own conscience.

Here, then, is my Memoir of that death, or perhaps I should say, at the risk of anticipating the difficult chronicle of those bygone deeds and days, of that crime. The following revelation of those events will cause the pious reader to shudder, not only at the premature and lamentable death of the Duchess, but also at its premeditated and cruel nature. To my recollection, that of an old man who, during the last thirty years of his life, has not been able to nurture anything other than that memory, deprived as he has been of all other action and enterprise, I add a report from the ministry of police, given additional importance by a Royal Order from my eminent

Lord Carlos IV immediately after the occurrence of the Duchess's death, and some letters I received many years later, during my exile in Rome, one in 1824 and the other in 1829, which complete, even in what they modify and refute, the impact of my recollection.

It has not been easy to write this text, which I will finally, some day, place before the reader's judgment. By their very nature, my earlier Memoirs obliged me to write in a formal style, elaborate and tedious, in keeping with the official and political nature of those volumes.[4] For this Brief Memoir, I propose a straightforward, more personal, more spontaneous language, for the sake of the testimony's authenticity, and as will be seen in more than one passage, thus diminish my dignity and my good name along with that of other persons, even more august, alluded to in this discourse.

Because of all this, and because of the repercussions that this may have on persons still living (including my own children) too intimately associated with the events or with its protagonists, I exhort that this Memoir be given no public disclosure until at least one hundred years after my death. This is my express will, which I pass on to my survivors, be they at the moment of my physical disappearance, my children, my grandchildren,[5] or my beloved and faithful wife, Josefa Tudó de Godoy, Countess of Castillofiel, my legal wife since the seventh day of January 1829 and therefore today, thanks to my belated reinstatement, also Duchess of Alcudia. I know that my family will respect my will, and I hope that their fidelity is passed on not only to my descendants but also to those in whose hands should fall, by the force of destiny on some distant day, this testament.[6]

D. Manuel de Godoy
Duke of Alcudia
Paris, 1848

Notes

1. The Decisive and Justificatory Memoirs for the History of the Reign of His Majesty Carlos IV de Borbón were in fact published by Godoy between the years 1836 and 1842 (in the original Spanish edition, they consisted of six volumes). Don Manuel dates this "Notice to the Reader" in 1848. We can infer that this new Memoir (called Brief only in keeping with a sense of proportion still typical of the Baroque) was written between the beginning of 1847 (Godoy, born in 1767, would have been in the "shadow of his eighties") and 1848.
2. Godoy's Memoirs were concluded in 1808 and included the Bayonne incident in which Carlos IV abdicated to Napoleon, or possibly covered only the few months after his fall. In those Memoirs, the author does not report any news of the Duchess's death, nor even mention the Duchess herself, not acknowledging therefore all the influence that such a notable, lively, and dauntless person had on public life in Carlos IV's Spain, as if by her eminently feminine, worldly, and passionate nature, she only deserved to figure in the chronicles of elegance or crime—or in the memoirs of art history, fatally linked to them as she always was.
3. In fact, by 1848, of the people implicated in some way in the Duchess's death, the only ones still living were Godoy, who died three years later, and Pepita Tudó, who did not die until 1868.
4. Many attribute that style—ornate, convoluted, ceremonial to the point of excess—more to the Abbot Sicilia, than to Godoy. Upon the recommendation of Martínez de la Rosa, Godoy entrusted the abbot with the final editing of his Memoirs. Sicilia, doubtless to expand the contract and thereby increase his profit, amused himself in that type of tortuous dropsy of style. It is appropriate

to recall in passing that Menéndez y Pelayo, self-styled historian of the Spanish language and eternal leader of the orthodox, rated the Spanish of the Memoirs "perverse."

5. Godoy had only one daughter by the Countess of Chinchón: Carlota, born in 1800 of the pregnancy Goya immortalized in his celebrated portrait. She was married in 1820 to the Italian noble, Count Ruspoli. However, some time before and through the intervention of her uncle, Cardinal Luis de Borbón, she was authorized by Fernando VII to use one of the titles seized from Godoy: Duchess of the Swedes. From his illegitimate union with Pepita Tudó, however, Godoy had at least two sons: Manuel and Carlos. The latter died at an early age in 1818, in Pisa, where papal diplomacy had forced Pepita to live to avoid a scandal in Rome, which her concubinage with Godoy would have caused. In 1848, the children of the other son, Manuel, were studying in Paris and living with their grandfather in his house on rue Neuve des Mathurins.

6. Don Manuel certainly could have had in mind *Don Álvaro, or the Force of Fate* by the Duke of Rivas, except that he translates *fate* as *destiny,* just as Verdi would do some fourteen years later and in Italian in his opera that, of course, Godoy did not get to enjoy. And so, "by the force of destiny," we have been the ones to defer publication of this interesting document until 1951, carrying out Don Manuel's testamentary will, although we had uncovered it many years before.* And may I add that I

---

*This is the only point at which the Marquis of Peñadolida reveals his intentions: to postpone publication of the Brief Memoir from 1939, the year in which he dates his "Notice," to 1951, when he was no longer in any condition to publish anything, obscurely buried as he was and is in Père-Lachaise. And, the "interesting document" would remain obscurely buried along with his own prologue, until I would find them by the renewed force of destiny.

cannot listen to the famous opening of Don Álvaro's duet in the second act ("*Solenne in quest'ora . . .* ") when some papers are entrusted to Don Carlos's care in just the same way, without imagining that Don Manuel is talking—or singing—to me from beyond the grave.

ROME, NOVEMBER 1824

I STARTED that day the way I always did. I left my quarters at the Villa Campitelli, which had seemed like a sad jail when I moved in five years before. Now I fancied them too spacious for my badly worn out and poorly managed solitude. I would have liked thed shouts and laughter of the children playing beyond my walls, in the garden or in the kitchens, to have reached those rooms more often.[1] I headed on foot toward the Pincio, not so much to stretch my legs but because my unstable economy forced me to. More and more, I did without a coach. I walked around the park for a half hour, enjoying the mild warmth of the autumn sun filtered by the pines, exchanging greetings with the same strangers I saw every morning. I bought a paper on the steps of the Piazza di Spagna, drank a hot chocolate in the Café Greco, talked about the weatherd with the waiter, found out the latest news from Paris, London, and Vienna, since *Il Messaggero* never concerned itself in the least with the official purge going on in Spain.[2] Returning in a rented coach, I looked over my mail.

My correspondence: every day, this was the most meticulously awaited event of a monotonous life, one barely engaged in the stimulation of surprise and emotion. I anxiously anticipated the contents of my letters, which later, if I had received any, I answered or not as I saw fit. In this setting, my anxiety was often dispelled in a fog of deception, in an entire afternoon spent busily answering those letters. Letters from Madrid, from my daughter, bringing me up to date on how my old demands were going at Court, on the King's ever negative reactions, on the unfinished lawsuits, on the eternal and wretched squandering and diminishing of the decisions that concerned my titles and my goods;[3] letters from Pisa, from Pepita, with, above all, news of our children's health (since Carlos's death, that was the constant focus of our worries) and with news, too, of her new Italian friends, of the rhythm of domestic life, of the cats and the servants, of the geraniums in her garden, where she was determined to revive the Cádiz of her childhood; letters, in the majority of cases, from London, from Lord Holland, or from Vienna, where the last of my friends were staying, the few who still wondered about me, no longer concerned about my destiny as a public man—they all seemed to agree on burying that forever—but rather about my distressing personal situation.

That is what my life had been reduced to. To waiting anxiously for letters that brought nothing new or at best only promises, advice, the illusion of distraction. To focusing on answering those letters, applying a powerful energy that long ago gave me more than enough strength to direct matters of state, to personally attend to my duties as minister sixteen hours a day. To joining in to everything the government of a nation and an empire offered: war, when it happened and—why not admit it, too?—love, which always happened. And here I was, still a long way from sixty, resigned to the equivalent of a correspondence between an old woman and her lawyer, parish priest, or her rich relative. A disheartening routine.

That day, however, the mail included an intriguing letter. It came from Bordeaux and was addressed (everyone had abandoned the custom by now) to "His Highness, the Prince of Peace, Don Manuel Godoy. . . ."

At first, I did not recognize the handwriting. Nevertheless something looked familiar in those large, slanting, nearly parabolic and in a certain way unrefined strokes. I studied it a long time before opening it. In Bordeaux, I knew, many exiled Spaniards lived . . . Moratín, Silvela, General Guerra. Iriarte, too? . . .[4] I did not correspond with any of them . . . But maybe . . . What flashes like lightning through the mind of a man in my position? Does the longing for action and power ever diminish? Are hopes really lost? I broke the sealing wax, tore open the envelope, looked for the signature. It read: Fr.co de Goya.

Goya. Don Fancho. El Maestro. Then he was still alive. He had survived. He had not succumbed to the catastrophe of Spain or to his last illness that five years earlier—the last I had heard any news of him—had brought him such terrible suffering. He was not crazy either, a man lost in a dream, the brim of his hat bristling with burning candles, wandering through the rooms of his villa in Manzanares, painting his bedeviled fantasies way into the night, the kind he had described to me long ago. None of that. He was in Bordeaux. In control of his faculties. Same as always. His handwriting had not lost the firm, boastful stroke with which, some thirty years ago, he had dared sign "Only Goya" at the feet of the

Duchess's portrait. Goya in Bordeaux. Old, unbeatable, unexpected.

The letter read:

My Highly Exalted Lord Don Manuel,

It should cause you not a little wonder that I address you as Your Highness* after so many years of separation and silence, and after so many unhappy events, such as have occurred in our beloved Spain. But I am recalling them for someone who has witnessed more of those events firsthand than I. And neither do I know if Y.H. had thought of me being in Bordeaux,[5] where I have just arrived with the Court's permission, a stay that I hope will be prolonged as long as I want it to be, and where I will be installed with my family until things change or until I die. I am now nearing eighty, Don Manuel, but I do not want to take up your time with my ailments.

The reason for this note is to find out if Y.H. has undertaken the business of writing your memoirs, work that I am very happy about because many lies and myths will be driven off with that work; my thinking is that I can contribute my grain of sand and modestly help you to meet those saintly ends, relating precious information to you regarding the lamentable event that occurred more than twenty years ago. I continue to conceal the truth of that event, when now it could not harm anyone should it be found out. Your keen wit will not fail

---

*For all his lofty and traditional address of me, aimed, I imagine, at setting a tone appropriate to the gravity of the subject, Goya composed his lines with such unconventional spelling, as the unschooled are wont to do, that I feel compelled to right that spelling for the ease of my readers.

to perceive which event I am referring to, since it involved us all. Without disclosure of this truth, people beloved and revered by Y.H. and by me will not ever be saved from the shadows surrounding them.

If Y.H. agrees with me and wants to obtain the private facts I know, to put them to a use that she would have deemed appropriate, I am ready to travel to Rome if need be—which will also be for me a nostalgic return to that city, after fifty years. While I do not believe that any of my friends from the days of my apprenticeship are still living, I would take advantage of the visit to study the treasures of the *belles artes* of Italy once again and to learn from them as I did before, that it is never too late to learn and I "still learn," as I say in one of my latest drawings,[6] and if Y. H. thinks as I do, you will, above all, want to learn from me what I so much want to tell you, so I can finally unburden my weary shoulders of the heavy weight of that distant and old history.

As a humble tribute I send to Y.H. this copy I have done of an old pencil drawing I never published. So that Y.H. can see for yourself that my hand does not tremble yet when I draw. My advice though if Y.H. would like to have a good portrait done today would be to go to Paris and have a young man named Delacroy paint it, or you might bring him to Rome. Would that we had someone like him in Spain, one I have admired in his own studio during my recent visit to that magnificent city. I am still learning, Don Manuel, even from the young people.[7]

Hoping you have a positive answer for me, telling me that we can see each other in Rome. Before beginning such a long trip, I take leave of Y.H. with a thousand greetings, memories, and happinesses that your most devoted friend and servant wishes for you,

Fr.co de Goya

I live in no. 7, on a street called Fossés de l'Intendance. And I am still learning.

I must confess that reading the letter did not get my attention first and foremost, as it should have. I did not immediately think about the old and mysterious event he alluded to, or the secret story of which Goya felt himself to be the trustee. Rather I submerged myself into more personal considerations, not free from irony. The old Maestro, despite his youthful and insistent disposal toward apprenticeship, was not very up-to-date in his facts about my circumstances. He still called me Prince, addressed me as Your Highness, imagined me in a position to travel to Paris for the sole pleasure of having my portrait done again, and even to bring his young and admired "Delacroy" to paint me with the Tivoli Gardens or a salon in the Barberini Palace as a backdrop.[8] Worse yet, he thought that my Memoirs were ready to be edited, when for the moment they were nothing more than a project, a vague plan deferred year after year, month after month, day after day, because, I suspect, something in me still resisted looking back to the past, closed and sealed, cut off. I resisted admitting that in some way Manuel Godoy had died in 1808, or at least a part of him, the public man that Spain and the world were prepared to remember and in doing so revile him. I stayed so wrapped up in these bitter thoughts that I did not even notice that the coachman had stopped in the Piazza del Popolo for some reason and had disappeared into the lively morning crowd. Mechanically, I unrolled the small cylinder of paper that had come inside a brass tube with the letter.

It was unmistakably a Goya drawing that could have without forcing or diminishing be included in his Capricho series.[9] It bore, as did the others, a caption in cursive, which said: *What Did the Dispirited Woman Die of?* As for the drawing, any of Goya's works are difficult to describe. In the catalogs of his work, this drawing probably figures in at the same height as all his Caprichos. But, as years before I had mislaid my copy and never learned what became of the original, any effort on my part to represent it in words would only be superfluous. The drawing has great movement, like a whirlwind or a spiral, and is composed of a central female figure, dressed in black and in a maja's mantilla; her face and arms are very white, her shoes sharply pointed. She flies—or tries to fly—while a mob of grotesque, evil monsters with large heads, undefined bodies and limbs, and menacing mouths tries to keep her from flying or, more likely, tries to cut her to pieces in midair, judging from the tension of the legs, the right arm of the woman and the aggressiveness of the monsters' hands and teeth. All that ripping and tearing turns to serenity and definitive flight in the woman's breast, in her placid and ironically smiling face, in her closed eyes and in her left arm, stretched out, like a wing free of hindrances, toward the sky, the snowy hand holding up a glass that, although turned gently upside down without any of the liquid spilling out, eventually would become empty. But the thing that impressed me most about the drawing was without a doubt not the startling contrast between the angelic placidity of the protagonist and the furious desires of the monsters, or even its value as fantasy, or the movement, or the composition, but that its translucent metaphor violently called to mind—as the letter had not managed to—the "lamentable event" to which the Maestro had obliquely referred: the grossly unjust death of an unequaled and captivating woman, the world of hate and malevolence that unfairly swooped down on her, the perfidious glass of poison that finally carried her off to a final peace.

But why the devil did that old, decrepit fool want to revive something in 1824 that had been buried in 1802? Why break a silence now that had not been a sovereign decree, but something of an understood pact we who had been close to Cayetana and to her death had woven among us that stifling and tragic summer? And what did Goya really know? The truth? Or was he boasting about something that was scarcely more than a new caprice of his imagination? Did he really think he had that old secret in his possession? And if he did, why not keep quiet about it? What did it matter to anyone now, except to him, who had loved her so much, and to the possible murderer. And to me, who was not going to include it in my Memoirs, me, who had found out how Cayetana really died? What if Goya had not kept quiet about it, then, like the rest of us? What if he had not accepted an official version certified by the royal seal itself from the chief of police like the rest of us? What if the Duchess's supporters, her heirs, for example, among whom figured a member of her own family, her chambermaid, and even her doctors, had not opted for circumspection and silence? Even the common people, worked up by rumors as if by a fleeting gale, hadn't they forgotten too?

I know that I posed these questions and repeated this entire rhetorical cascade to my myself that afternoon, pacing about my chambers at Villa Campitelli, refusing to eat, despite Magdalena's solicitude and pressures, reading Goya's letter again and again, which said so much and so little, and above all trying to find in the drawing—in the face of that Sphinx of a woman, the maja-duchess, in the glass at once mortal and savior, in that script, well-formed, elongated, and English—an answer to to the question "What did the dispirited woman die of?" that left the terrifying answer hanging in the air. And today, more than four lustrums later, I ask myself if age or death's approach—the same thing, of course—made Goya then, the way it makes me today, tell the truth, our truths, different one from another but equally compelling regarding the "lamentable event." So, that someone today could ask himself with the same bitterness the way I did when I rebelled that afternoon: Why would that old, decrepit fool want to revive halfway through the century something that was buried in that century's dawning?

That very night, at the opera, with my daughter's Italian in-laws, the Ruspolis, who limited their social contact with me to three or four gestures of courtesy a year, the most frequent of which were invitations to their theater box, I attended a production of *Lucrezia Borgia* by Gaetano Donizetti, one of my favorite composers in those days. I had forced myself to accept their invitation, largely because it came in the middle of that afternoon upset by Goya's letter, as a providential way to avoid the exaggerated and growing alarm that that letter had provoked in me. But I was mistaken in my calculations. Not even the young musician's splendid lyrics, the sweet, sweet voices of the soprano and the tenor, or the far from androgenous enchantments of the young woman who played Count Orsini managed to carry me to that heaven of distraction and oblivion that I had forecast for myself. I continued, obsessively, immersed in that other mysterious heaven where Don Fancho's maja was flying, goblet in hand, trying to escape the claws of those ugly demons; I followed that white and featureless image, scarcely a symbol of the soul more than of the body, that was superimposed to the point of excluding the very details of my recollections of Cayetana, blurred and confused in its most remote embodiment. What's worse, from the first act, the opera seemed to speak and sing about nothing else but poison. In the glass and the flask that at the end passed between the hands of Lucrezia and her son, it seemed a hallucination to me. I seemed to be seeing the crystal Venetian glass in the maja's left hand, so faithfully reproduced in Goya's drawing. It was, my God, yes, the very same smalt goblet that I still remembered with the candlelight shining bright in the crystal and in the amber liquid, sitting on Cayetana's dressing table. The glass in Lucrezia's hands shines, and I suddenly see Cayetana—or is it only a Goya-esque illustration?—raising the glass to her lips. I sat bolt upright, let out a muffled groan, like those that in the middle of the night wrench us from a nightmare to exorcise our ghosts. I see the large, alarmed face of a chimera, Signora Ruspoli's face, turn toward me, the stage lights in the background, and her husband, who leans over solicitously and asks *sotto voce* through his mustache: "What's the matter, Don Manuel?"[10]

I drank a bottle of Frascati, thinking it would help me sleep and went straight to bed, not even glancing over at the letter or the drawing. But I could not get to sleep. Visions of the real Cayetana—Cayetana the evening of her death, wearing that flame-colored dress, incandescent, her face already wan and gritty from her last years, disguised by cunning makeup—still struggled to open the way behind the nearly abstract face in the drawing, the white oval, the slight curve of the mouth, the two small, dark half-circles of eyelids between the arc of her black eyebrows and the dotted line of her lowered eyelashes. With that succession of visions, I did not try to go to sleep. On top of all that, vicious, twisting, warped monsters were mixed in—a mass of horror and brutality ready to spring on me in my dream. I climbed out of bed, grabbed up an old lamp that was still lit and went into my study. There I kept, among my new papers, the few old papers that first Murat and then my son-in-law had managed to save from the pillage and the confiscation.[11] I was not mistaken. The document I was looking for was there, the scrambled pages, yellowed and cast aside. In the silence of the night, barely disturbed by a far-off nightingale or the sound of old trees creaking in the wind, I read the report.

Notes

1. By January 1819, María Luisa had died in Rome and Carlos IV, in Naples. Godoy had to leave the Barberini Palace, where he had been living with them, and take refuge in Villa Campitelli, a mansion that he had given to Socorro Tudó, Pepita's sister, and where Socorro and a third sister, Magdalena, had moved with their respective families. The children who were playing "beyond the walls"—surrounding what Godoy calls "his quarters" and which were just one part of the villa—could be none other than Socorro's and Magdalena's children.
2. This may be a good time to refresh the reader's memory about the Spain of 1824. After the invasion by the One Hundred Thousand Sons of San Luis, sent by Louis XVIII in 1823 to restore Fernando VII to the throne and the execution in the same year of Rafael de Riego y Núñez for leading the resistance to that campaign, the Crown's response had grown fiercer than ever. Goya, himself a very important person in this story, came to fear for his freedom. Between January and April 1824, feeling threatened by possible denunciation, he sought

refuge in the home of a canon. In May he requested permission from the King to move to Plombières, France, allegedly to take the medicinal baths.

3. These negotiations, which involved the Spanish embassy in Rome and the papal chancellery, did not culminate until six years later, when Godoy, already a widower from the Countess of Chinchón and married to Pepita Tudó, exchanged his prized and litigious title of Prince of Peace for the fief of Bassano, next to Sutri, whose owner was traditionally granted the status of Roman prince by the Pope. For this honor Godoy had to pay seventy thousand piasters, in addition to renouncing his Spanish title. Until 1823, the year of his death, Godoy's brother-in-law, the Cardinal, Don Luis de Borbón, archbishop of Toledo, always negotiated lawsuits and demands on Godoy's behalf. Then Carlota, Godoy's daughter, took over. She ended up bringing legal action herself against her father many years later on a question of property.

4. Moratín, Silvela, and General Guerra did live in Bordeaux in 1824, and Pío Molina, General Pastor, Don Dámaso de la Torre, the painter Brugada, as well. But not Iriarte, who had died ten years earlier in 1814, something Godoy did not know in 1824 or had forgotten in 1848.

5. Arriving from Spain, Goya went through Bordeaux, stayed in Paris for two months, and was not settled in Bordeaux until October. In November, when he wrote the letter to Godoy, he was already petitioning Fernando VII for an extension of his permission, always under the pretext of the alleged water cure.

6. Barely arrived in France, Goya drew his famous *I Am Still Learning* in the throes of his latest French discoveries: the technique of lithography and the genius of Delacroix himself. Until then the drawing was vaguely dated in the "Bordeaux period" (1824–1828), but Goya's letter settles that question.

7. This part of the letter confirms something that until now was only wishful thinking by art historians: That Goya not only saw the paintings of the young Delacroix during his stay in Paris, which coincided with the exposition of the younger painter's great *Massacre of Chios* in the Salon in 1824, but that he knew Delacroix as well, spent time in his workshop, and appreciated his art.
8. Godoy did live in the Barberini Palace with the King and Queen from his arrival in Rome until their deaths. His reference to the Tivoli Gardens, more enigmatic, is perhaps nothing more than a literary flourish, or an indication of personal taste. Regarding the titles, Godoy seems to have already given up using them, although he continued petitioning Fernando VII for his right to use them.
9. This drawing that Goya sent to Godoy and which, despite anecdotal differences seems so much like the famous *Volaverunt*, has disappeared. This makes one think that the misplacement of the copy and the destruction of the original can be attributed to the same cause. It is impossible to know in any case if this drawing corresponds to a drawing that in 1828, after the painter's death, was identified with the number fifteen in the inventory of his belongings, as "Two Caprichos, sketches." One might surmise that the sketch that interests us was indeed one of them and that some interested hand made it disappear or still keeps it today out of the public eye and out of the catalog of Goya's work.
10. This is one of the most flagrant errors in Don Manuel's memoirs—brief or long. He cannot have attended a production of *Lucrezia Borgia* in November 1824, in Rome, because Donizetti had not written it yet and would not produce it until 1833, at La Scala, in Milan. Either Godoy deliberately changed the facts, confused two operas with similar peripeteia, or confused that opera performance in Rome with some later performance at the Paris Opéra, in which he fused the poison and

the glass of his memories with the poison and glass of Donizetti's story.

11. In his Memoirs, Godoy himself alludes to the nearly total confiscation and later disappearance of his books and private papers and to those papers that Murat, Napoleon's general, was able to save and return to him. The removal and concealment of documents, whether out of treachery or not, mark these brief Memoirs, the criminal fact they refer to, and in general everything concerning the life and death of Cayetana de Alba. It is as if Godoy had wanted to sweep from posterity all information that was not the ambiguous and enigmatic profile in Goya's portraits and drawings. Not even those drawings would be saved from the Inquisition's excesses, as we suggested in note nine in this same chapter.

MADRID, JULY-AUGUST 1802

Report from the Ministry of Police

In the city of Madrid, the thirty-first day of Our Lord, July 1802, in accordance with a Royal Order from His Majesty Don Carlos IV, issued the twenty-eighth day of the same month in his palace of La Granja and communicated to these precincts by His Excellency Lord Prime Minister Don Manuel Godoy, Prince of Peace, for its effective and swift execution, an investigation was begun into the cause of the death of Doña María del Pilar Teresa Cayetana de Silva y Álvarez de Toledo, Duchess of Alba, on the twenty-third day of Our Lord of this same month at her domicile in the city of Madrid. The order was carried out in accordance with the following procedures: The chief of police himself accompanied by two detectives presented themselves at said residence, known as the palace of Buenavista, located on the site of the former gardens of Juan Hernández, having an entrance on Empress Street but no house number, and proceeded to inquire into the case, inspecting the scene of the events and interrogating all persons who could furnish reliable information concerning said demise.

In the absence of close family members, the Duchess of Alba being widowed with no descendants, her parents deceased, and she being an only child, Lady Doña Catalina Barajas, her chambermaid, and Don Ramón Cabrera, her chaplain, receive us and place themselves at our disposal. They advise us to contact Don Carlos Pignatelli, a member of the deceased's family, whom they offer to summon personally to talk with us. While we await the arrival of the aforementioned, who does not dwell in the palace but rather in his own residence on Barquillo Street, we ask the chaplain, who is working in the palace oratory, to be on hand for questioning.

Srta. Barajas turns out to be, in addition to chambermaid, the person among the Duchess's entire staff closest to her mistress during the years she has been in the lady's service and, due to the intimacy of her duties and by her own testimony, the person who was with the late Duchess at the time of her death, the first to witness the Duchess's malaise, the one who helped her the evening before, and the one who was mainly with her during the hours that elapsed until her death.

Srta. Barajas leads us to the Duchess's private quarters, located on the top floor, separated from the rest of the residence by various empty rooms (one of them walled with mirrors), as yet unincorporated into palace life as they are under construction and without fitting decoration; only one of those rooms has any character, the provisional studio of the painter Don Francisco de Goya, who, on the orders of her ladyship, the Duchess, was in the process of decorating those rooms. The Duchess's quarters are made up of three rooms: an antechamber for receiving guests and for dressing, a suite with a bedroom, and a boudoir with all the modern conveniences. The owner of these quarters did not leave them the last twelve hours of her life, the time that elapsed from the first symptoms of her illness until her death. Eight days having passed since this occurrence and five since her funeral, we find the rooms straightened and closed up; Srta. Barajas has personally seen to this task; Srta. Barajas did not find anything of special note in these quarters. Srta. Barajas points out to us that these quarters have only one door to the rest of the palace, the one that joins the antechamber to the main hallway, making it difficult for any outsiders to gain access to the owner's rooms or to her personal staff or servants.

We proceed to question Srta. Barajas. The following is a report of our findings:

Question: Name?

Answer: Catalina Barajas Carneiro.

Q: Relationship to the deceased?

A: I am . . . I was her chambermaid.

Q: You are or you were?

A: Forgive me. I was. My lady is dead. She doesn't need me anymore.

Q: How long have you carried out those duties?

A: All my life.

Q: Since you two were children?

A: Forgive me. I'll try to be more precise. I have been in the Duchess's service since before she was married. I was practically a child. I don't remember my exact age, forgive me. When she married the Duke, I stayed by her side. I was one of her maids. I've been employed as chambermaid since my predecessor's retirement, some eight years ago.

Q: You're not certain of the exact day?

A: Yes, I am. Saint Catherine's Day, 1794. Her Ladyship wanted to give me a present on my saint's day. She was very generous and thought a lot about others.

Q: And when was the last time you saw the Duchess alive?

A: She died in my arms.

Q: Did she suffer a great deal?

A: Quite a bit. But in the last moments she was calm.

Q: Did she say anything before she died that would be of interest to this investigation?

A: She said . . . Forgive me. I don't think you would be interested.

Q: We'll decide what's important.

A: She said, "My dear Catalina, that scoundrel death is waving to me, like a bullfighter with his cape. I'm off . . ."

Q: What do you think caused her death?

A: Her own doctors can't reach an agreement. Some kind of fever, they say. That could be it. We had just gotten back from Andalucía; we saw many dying people there. Her symptoms weren't the same, though. I really don't know. And now it doesn't matter . . .

Q: Let us decide what matters and what doesn't. Do you have any reason to believe that the Duchess could have died from something besides an illness?

A: I don't understand, sir.

Q: Something besides natural causes . . . premeditated . . . Poison, maybe. Let's say, murder.

A: God deliver me from that thought! My heart would grow cold with hate!

Q: Forget those feelings for now. Do you or don't you think that it's possible she may have drunk poison without knowing it?

A: But that would be dreadful!

Q: Do you want me to ignore the rumor going around Madrid?

A: I haven't been out on the streets, sir. We in the palace, we've done nothing but cry. None of us has thought about poison, I assure you. We accept the designs of Providence. However hard they may be to understand. They've cut down a marvelous human being in the prime of her life: my mistress.

Q: You don't know of anyone with a grudge against the Duchess, someone who would try to hurry her death along?

A: No one, sir. Here in the palace we all loved her. Outside the palace . . . you know more about that than I. Still I can't believe that . . .

Q: Did your mistress receive any visitors the day before her death?

A: Several, the evening before. She gave a party. There were sixteen people at the table. Sr. Pignatelli or the secretary, Sr. Berganza, could give you the names. I was in the kitchen, directing the help.

Q: Is that part of your duties?

A: My duties were to do all my lady required of me. And she had a great deal of confidence in me.

Q: Did you see the Duchess after the party?

A: Of course. She called me to her room. I always help her . . . forgive me, I used to help her undress.

Q: Did she seem to be in a normal frame of mind?

A: The way she usually was after parties. A little sad, a little restless.

Q: Did she say or do anything unusual?

A: No. Well . . . She offered me a glass of wine. They had given us some sherry during our trip to Andalucía, and she had a bottle in her dressing room. It's still there; you must have seen it.

Q: Did you drink some?

A: We both did. It's an exquisite wine.

Q: When did the Duchess start to show signs of feeling ill? In the morning?

A: No. An hour or two later. I had fallen asleep. She called me in again. Nausea, cold sweats, abdominal pains . . . A little while later, we sent someone for the doctor. Dr. Bonells arrived. By then, it was morning.

The first interview ended. Don Carlos Pignatelli was now in the palace. Sr. Pignatelli turns out to be a prominent young man, with bold manners and a quick wit. Srta. Barajas makes a parlor with a desk on the first floor available to us. She tells us can use it for as long as we need to during the investigation. We have called Sr. Pignatelli to that room. The following is a record of that interview:

Question: Name?

Answer: Carlos Pignatelli y Alcántara.

Q: Relationship to the deceased?

A: That's hard to explain. Above all, you could call it an old and deep friendship. But we were related by an unusual sort of legal guardianship, since my father, Count de Fuentes's, second marriage to the Duchess's mother. You could say, that made us brother and sister, but that relationship was so curious we might as well have been married. Pretty complicated I know . . . To simplify things, we used to call each other cousins. Cousin Carlos. Cousin Cayetana.

Q: Did you see her often?

A: At the beginning, fairly often. Our parents were married on the same day she married the Duke. We belonged to the same world, we were the same age—well, she was just a little bit older than I—we went to the same parties, we enjoyed the same activities. Then I was gone for a few years, living in Paris. When I came back, we both had changed and she was a widow. Since then I have been a frequent visitor—first at the palace at Moncloa and now, here in Buenavista. I became, I think, a kind of a companion. The French have a word for it: *chevalier servant.* Not an intimate relationship, you understand.

Q: When was the last time you saw her?

A: Alive? I suppose that's what you're interested in. About an hour before she succumbed to death, when I went out again to find Don Francisco Durán, one of her personal physicians. (I say again because we had been trying in vain to find him . . .) I finally found him and brought him to the palace. She died a little while later. Horrible. I couldn't believe it. My cousin had been so full of life, full of spirit . . . Forgive me, you didn't ask me about that.

Q: What do you think caused her death?

A: The doctors can answer that better than I can, I suppose. I don't believe in doctors very much, although of course I run to get them whenever someone needs them.

Q: Do you have any reason to suspect anything other than natural causes in your cousin's death?

A: Poison? I should've guessed; it's inevitable. I mean: You police always think that way . . . Well, no, I have no reason to suspect that. Though there's no reason to rule it out either . . .

Q: Just answer the question, please. Let's take this one step at a time. Did poison cross your mind when you saw the Duchess get sick so quickly?

A: I'll try to answer just that question. No. No, poison did not cross my mind. First I thought about her crazy trip to Andalucía . . .

Q: So you blame some illness on that trip . . .

A: I don't blame anything on anything. I'm no doctor. Go ask one of them. Please. But everyone warned her not to make that trip, with disease everywhere, and so on and so forth. But as usual, she did what she pleased.

Q: Then, would you say that if the deceased hadn't taken that trip, she wouldn't have come down with that illness that took her life in a few short hours?

A: You keep insisting! What do you want me to say? God knows! If an important person like her wanted to go and expose herself to disease, it's her business! My cousin hadn't been well for a long time. Some disease was aging her, wearing her down . . . If some disease came on suddenly, it found fertile ground to thrive in.

Q: Then someone could have planned to speed up the process?

A: What do you mean? Murder, again! Of course, you can't rule it out. Exceptional people are a great source of irritation for the mediocre, sir. And cousin Cayetana was exceptional. But, of course, you would have to come up with a mediocre person with the makings of a murderer.

Q: Let's go to something more concrete. The Duchess gave a party the night she died. Tell us about it.

A: Here. I've made a list while I was waiting. I took it for granted you'd ask me for it. Sixteen people altogether, including the hostess. An intimate gathering, but there were guests for every taste: from a landed prince to an actor. Read it. It's a spectrum of my cousin's social life.

Q: We'll read it in due time. Right now can you tell us if the Duchess ate or drank anything during the party that the guests didn't have?

A: Sr. Chief of Police, in our world eating or drinking anything that is not offered to one's guests is considered a serious lack of manners.

Q: That's all for now, Sr. Pignatelli.

The list of diners the night of the Duchess's death includes the following people: Don Fernando, Prince of Asturias; General Duke of Alcudia and Prince of Peace, Don Manuel de Godoy and his wife, the Countess of Chinchón; the Archbishop of Toledo, Don Luis de Borbón; the Count-Duke of Benavente-Osuna; Count Haro and his fiancée, Doña Manuela Silva y Waldstein; General Eusebio Cornel; Doña Pepita Tudó; Don Carlos Pignatelli; Don Francisco de Goya, painter; Don Isidoro Máiquez, actor; Doña Rita Luna, actress; and Don Manuel Costillares, bullfighter. Don Manuel Godoy and his wife departed at approximately two A.M.; everyone else, two hours later. After seeing the other guests out on the hostess's behalf, Sr. Pignatelli himself retired to his home. There seems to be no reason to bring any of these people in for questioning since the Duchess of Alba was in good health until the end of the party, which proceeded quite normally.

However, we are interested in the testimony of the two doctors who attended the deceased during her agony. We ask Sr. Pignatelli to contact them for a meeting with us the following afternoon. Meanwhile, we took a sample from the bottle of sherry so a chemist could analyze it.

On August 1, 1802, we arrived at six P.M. at the Buenavista Palace. There we found Don Jaime Bonells and Don Francisco Durán, the deceased's personal physicians, waiting for us. Dr. Bonells is a very old man, with the mannerisms, outlook, and discretion associated with doctors of the old school; Dr. Durán is young, energetic, and arrogant, and belongs to the new class of surgeons, educated in the concepts of medicine in vogue at the universities in France and England. We start by questioning the older of the two.

Question: Name?

Answer: Jaime Bonells Sunyer.

Q: Relationship to the deceased?

A: I am honored to have been the personal physician for the distinguished Alba family for more than forty years. I have treated the Duchess since she joined the family in 1775 and I attended the Duke, her husband, in his last hours.

Q: What about the Duchess's last moments, last July 23?

A: I did not have that honor. In those hours my colleague, Don Francisco Durán, replaced me. A very talented, young surgeon, let me say.

Q: Then, she was in good hands?

A: From the moment she was in his hands, needless to say.

Q: So, you didn't treat the Duchess during the suffering that took her life?

A: I have not expressed myself clearly. Please forgive me. I was called to the Duchess's bedside very early in the morning, and I stayed at her side some nine hours, trying to remedy her condition. Without success I am ashamed to say. It was not God's will.

Q: Then, you were her personal physician?

A: Please let me explain. I was and I wasn't. I attended the Duchess continually up until about four years ago. Then she put herself in Dr. Durán's care. I remained at her beck and call. I could do no less; it was my moral duty to continue coming to the palace whenever they called upon me to treat family members and servants. But I, personally, did not treat the Duchess again except for some slight cold or constipation, and anytime my colleague was out of town.

Q: Then why were you called that morning?

A: I wasn't told exactly. I presume they first sent for Don Francisco, but they couldn't find him. Old Bonells is always around when you need him and is quick to help anyone—and even quicker to treat the Duchess herself—as the medical vocation and Christian morals command him to do.

Q: Are you suggesting that the other doctor could have failed to do that?

A: For God's sake! I did not say that. Dr. Durán, who I repeat deserves all my respect, professionally speaking, must have had his reasons for not getting here right away.

Q: What was your diagnosis of the Duchess's illness?

A: You've touched a nerve, Inspector. Since I had not visited my patient for four years, I was not in the best position to diagnose her condition. At first I considered an intoxication like those miasmas of summer that manage to get a hold on us. But when I learned that the Duchess, against all recommendations, including mine, had insisted on traveling to Andalucía, when I learned from Doña Catalina that she had been around the ill, I was inclined to think that she had contracted one of those terrible fevers, that that fever had incubated for several days, and finally it had shown up at the time it seemed to afflict her.

Q: Do you think, like everyone else, that the Duchess was wasting away, her body weakened, susceptible to disease?

A: The Duchess was a vigorous woman. She was not even forty yet. Now, if she was suffering from old illnesses not thoroughly or conscientiously treated, I cannot be the judge of that . . . Dr. Durán, who treated her these last years, could tell you that better than I. I limited myself to doing what was put in my hands, and I should say that God's will wanted me to fail. When I learned that Don Francisco had announced his arrival, I went home to avoid interventions and suspicions that, from the bottom of my heart, I abhor.

Q: Did you at any time think that the Duchess could have been poisoned?

A: What are you saying?! Not for a minute. And by whom? My God! Those things don't happen in the Alba household. We are in Spain, Inspector, and despite the evil that surrounds us, nothing goes against the Spanish soul more than a weapon as traitorous and treacherous as poison. No, I flatly reject that insinuation.

Q: Then, do you reject the idea that someone might have had a reason to do away with the Duchess?

A: Why would anyone have such an idea? She was the Duchess of Alba! She may have had her flaws; we all do. Perhaps she was a bit moody and given to crazy ideas and therefore inclined to flights of fancy (I am referring to some forms of quackery). But you don't poison someone for that, sir! And besides that, a doctor of my long experience would have detected symptoms of poisoning right away and would have combated them correctly, and if he was unsuccessful, would have demanded an autopsy. This did not happen. That is the best answer I can give you.

We dismissed Dr. Bonells, who was a bit upset at the end of the questioning. We called Don Francisco Durán. The two doctors met and greeted each other coldly but civilly. The young surgeon sat down and began to ask questions. We had to remind him that he was there to answer questions. The following is the record of our questioning:

Question: Name?
Answer: Francisco Durán y Conde.
Q: Relationship to the deceased?
A: I've been her surgeon since the beginning of 1798.
Q: Taking Dr. Jaime Bonells's place?
A: Did Bonells tell you that? Poor old man. For him it was an insult, and he can't get over it. Did he criticize me?
Q: Please, Dr. Durán. I repeat. We'll ask the questions. Testimony is strictly confidential.
A: Fine. Fine. I understand. So much the better. Let's not make this any longer than it has to be. Ask your questions.
Q: Why did you start treating the Duchess?
A: Oh, the usual. A recommendation. I successfully treated one of the Benavente-Osuna children. The Duchess was bothered by some headaches that weren't responding to treatment . . . Well, to get to the point: Old Bonells didn't have a clue. I did. It isn't a big skill. Chance and educated guesses play a role in the development of medicine. It's an art still in its infancy; one should remember that.
Q: Did you know that your patient, the Duchess, had a debilitating disease, given to . . . ?

A: That is too broad a diagnosis. More what a layman, not a man of science, would say. The Duchess responded well to some of my treatments, poorly to others. She was close to forty, I believe. An age when nature has already given up some spans of its terrain to death.

Q: Do you have a clear idea of what caused her sudden and—let's say—violent death?

A: Keep one thing in mind. I got there when she was already dying. You know that her family summoned me all day, but I had gone hunting and had not returned yet . . . A regrettable circumstance. Perhaps something could have been done. Given the state I found her in, it was better to let her die peacefully.

Q: Do you believe she could have died from something other than natural causes?

A: What do you mean? Come out and say it.

Q: Poison . . .

A: For God's sake! Now I see. How melodramatic! Poison? Why not? On the other hand, why? There is no scientific proof that would lead us to that conclusion. That's a hypothesis . . . from plays, from novels! But I don't have enough scientific reasons to rule it out, either. Want the truth? To me that idea's worth as much as those Madrid miasmas or those Andalusian diseases . . . Every idea is worth something. On the other hand, they may just be good guesses without evidence to back them up . . . But we aren't going to subject the poor Duchess to an autopsy with so little evidence, are we? Then let's make do with the medical report, the one Bonells and I agreed on and signed: "We certify the death etcetera, etcetera of Doña María Teresa etcetera, etcetera caused by some intestinal disorder that she contracted etcetera, etcetera . . .

Q: Thank you, Dr. Durán. You may go.

A: Oh, by the way. That good woman, Catalina, has just informed us that this afternoon we are to go to the lawyer's office for the reading of the Duchess's will. Apparently she has left us an inheritance. Bonells, too. I hope she didn't leave him less than me. He couldn't take it. He has very high blood pressure. You feel tempted to give him a blood letting. If you come tomorrow, Sr. Detective, perhaps we may have something to celebrate together. The Duchess was extremely generous. But, I'm sure, each one of us would rather have her in the palace still singing and running around. Poison? Melodramatics, gentlemen.

Q: You may go, Dr. Durán.

On the second of August we got the report from the chemist on the sherry: negative. It turned out to be the highest quality sherry, not tampered with in any way. All the contents were used up in the tests, so the bottle was returned empty to the Duchess's boudoir. We arrived at the Buenavista Palace at the same time as the day before. Don Carlos Pignatelli showed us in. Six other people were with him: Srta. Catalina Barajas; Dr. Jaime Bonells, and Dr. Francisco Durán, whose testimony we have already heard in their respective questioning; Don Ramón Cabrera, chaplain; Don Tomás de Berganza, secretary; and Don Antonio Bargas, the Duchess's valet and treasurer. All seven of them wanted to tell us formally that they had been named equal heirs to the Duchess's entire estate and that they all wanted to put themselves at our disposal for the best outcome of the investigation. At the same time, they asked that it be carried out in such a way that it would not fan the flames of rumors that were going around town (that they considered totally unfounded, although they depended on the outcome of our inquest to confirm that) and that it not sully the memory of their illustrious and beloved benefactress with unnecessary scandal. We must point out that Sr. Pignatelli, who spoke for the rest, showed himself to be more willing to help us than in his previous questioning, and that Dr. Bonells and Dr. Durán said repeatedly that they had conferred and had agreed completely that poison and an autopsy could be ruled out. The three people who had not yet undergone our questioning stayed in the palace on our orders, which we proceeded to carry out. First, we called the chaplain.

Question: Name?

Answer: Ramon Cabrera Pérez.

Q: Relationship to the deceased?

A: I was in charge of the palace chapel, just as I was in charge of the chapel at Moncloa, and the various private oratories in her homes and palaces when the deceased traveled to her other estates.

Q: You were also her confessor?

A: On occasion.

Q: Are you saying that the Duchess did not keep the sacraments?

A: Not at all, sir. It is not my place to tell you what you have asked me. Those are private matters between a person and God. We priests are no more than intermediaries of a . . .

Q: When was the last time you saw the Duchess on religious matters?

A: The last minutes of her life. I was able to give her the last rites. Extreme Unction.

Q: What would you attribute her death to?

A: God wanted to call her to His bosom. Natural causes . . . illness, let's say . . . Well, I don't know. You have already heard what the doctors say. I saw her four or five times during the course of her suffering, to help her in her prayers. God subjected her to a hard test. Waves of pain came one after another. She could barely finish a Hail Mary. At the end she was weak and calm, as if the illness had taken place so her soul could fly to God more freely.

Q: Didn't you form any idea about what caused her suffering?

A: That was the doctor's concern. My attention had to be on the other side. All agony has two faces. Agony, in Greek, means struggle. And the struggle is double: One deals with the health of the body and that is the doctor's concern; the other deals with the soul's salvation, and that is the only thing that should concern a priest caring for a dying person.

Q: Didn't you consider even for a moment that the Duchess could have been poisoned?

A: My answer is implicit in what I have just told you. It didn't cross my mind. But now that you bring it up, now that that seems to be reason for conjecture and commentary around here, I can tell you that I strongly reject the idea. Now please understand me; priests are not afraid of evil. We are all of us more familiar with it than other mortals are. But in this case, considering poison seems to me a typical worldly perversion. In these times of so much impiety surrounding us, God's mysterious plans are not accepted as sufficient cause. People have to explain everything, the way those devils, those demons of rationalism would like everything to be.

Q: Thank you, Father. One last question. Do you know of anyone who'd want to harm the Duchess?

A: One should never seek enemies outside one's self, sir. Enemies lie in wait for us in our own soul. The Duchess had hers, naturally! Like the rest of us. Pride, vanities, matters of the flesh . . . Those are the poisons! Those are the poisoners!

Q: That will be all, Father. Thank you for your cooperation. Please tell Sr. Berganza to come in.

Old Father Cabrera, who seems to have few years of mental health left to enjoy his new inheritance, has Sr.

Berganza come in. He's a young man, slight and fidgety, who from the minute he arrives seems ready to answer our questions.

Question: Name?

Answer: Tomás de Berganza y García de Zúñiga.

Q: Relationship to the deceased?

A: Private secretary, for three years. But for a long time before that the Duchess had been my patron, ever since I lost my father, when I was barely six. The Duchess protected me, arranged my education, paid for my studies, put me on her staff. Everything I am I owe to her.

Q: What kind of work did you do?

A: I filed her correspondence and answered it when it wasn't strictly private. I kept a *pour memoire* of her social engagements, dealt with certain types of visitors, did some of her shopping—all and all, things that required a confidence you can place in someone with the same tastes and viewpoints . . . To give you an idea, at the party that night, I was busy arranging the seating at the table, buying flowers, hiring the musicians and choosing their music: Boccherini, Haydn, Corelli. See? A thousand details. It was a wonderful life. Without her things will never be the same, in spite of her incomparable generosity . . .

Q: When did you see her for the last time?

A: The night of the party, at the beginning and at some point when I went up to see if everything was going right. And it was. It was an unforgettable party. The Duchess looked splendid that night, in her flame-colored dress. Who would have guessed that a few hours later . . . Forgive me, I can't remember that night without . . .

Q: You didn't see her during her suffering?

A: I didn't want to, I couldn't. I was too upset. I wouldn't have been able to control myself in front of her. Everyone agreed that it was better if I didn't go in . . . And I wanted to keep that last memory of her.

Reigning over the party! A goddess! That's what she was. A goddess.

Q: What do you think the Duchess died of?

A: My God, she was so delicate, so frail, it could've been anything . . . And in Andalucía, she was foolish and exposed herself to disease in spite of everyone's warning. Do you know she sat up all night with a poor gypsy man afflicted with those horrible fevers? There was no way to talk her out of it. Finally we were able to drag her back to Madrid . . . And for what, my God for what? For this tragic end . . . Forgive me, you're getting impatient. What did she die of? I'd say she caught the fever . . . But aren't you going to ask me about poison?

Q: Let's talk about that.

A: What can I tell you? Who can say? Poison, yes, it is a tragic end for a marvelous life . . . It almost . . . makes sense, doesn't it? Yet, when could anyone have given it to her? During the party? Would someone have dared poison her glass in plain view of everyone? And who? One of the guests? My God! Have you seen the list? The royal family itself, a cardinal, the Osunas . . . and the others: Goya, Costillares, the Máiquezes, they adored her . . . Then, who? Who?

Q: You tell us, Sr. Berganza. Who?

A: A monster. Someone who envied her and wanted to end a life so rich and brilliant as hers . . . That's it, a monster. You'd have to look for a monster, Sr. Chief of Police.

Q: Thank you for your cooperation, Sr. Berganza. You can go now.

A: Shall I tell Sr. Bargas to come in?

Q: Please.

Sr. Bargas is a man well along in years, dressed in black, with a certain parsimonious air, the look of a shyster. When he comes in to testify, his dark mood instantly disperses the somewhat feverish and effervescent atmosphere left by Sr. Berganza. He sits down in silence and rarely raises his gray eyes above his pince-nez.

Question: Name?
Answer: Antonio Bargas.
Q: Bargas what?
A: Bargas Bargas.
Q: Relationship to the deceased?
A: I was her valet and treasurer. I served the late Duke as well.
Q: When did you see the deceased for the last time?
A: A few hours before her death. I was in her antechamber. I didn't want to go in. I thought I would bother her. She had them summon me. She wanted to see me.
Q: Did she have something to tell you?
A: I thought that despite her malaise, she wanted to settle some business with me as she did every day. But I only had to look at her to understand that that was impossible. The poor little Duchess . . . Forgive me. To me she was always the little Duchess; I met her when she was almost a girl, on her wedding day. But, the Duchess was dying. I understood right away.
Q: So, why did she send for you? To tell you good-bye?
A: Perhaps. Perhaps that too. Poor little dear. But she wanted to tell me something: the name of the lawyer with whom she had left her will on deposit.
Q: To what causes do you attribute the Duchess's death?
A: I rely on what the doctors say. Everything else seems like idle talk to me.
Q: And you never considered for a moment some external cause, some . . . ?
A: Poison? Not for an instant. Fantasies of the idle.
Q: Do you know of anyone who wanted to harm the Duchess?

A: No one. A few were a little jealous, at the most. But someone wanting to do what you say, no one. She was a frank, straightforward, generous woman. She disarmed everyone, even the most reluctant.

Q: You can go, Sr. Bargas. And thank you.

A: Thank you.

Sr. Bargas left, staying behind a moment to wipe his glasses, and with his testimony . . .*

---

*My study of this document was obstructed here. One or two of the last pages of the report are missing, I think, with inferences that their contents do not vary greatly. The hypothesis of poison was rejected because of a lack of evidence, because the doctors' reports were in agreement, and above all because of a lack of an apparent motive. This theory was attributed to be the fruit of popular imagination and Court slander, both brought to a head in the reigning dog days.
M.G.

ROME, NOVEMBER 1824

(continued)

It was half past four in the morning when I finished reading the police report. The gravity and vividness of those memories, the nearly physical recollection, with a warmth and perfume all its own, of a night like that one and a report like that one, twenty-two years before, was the same, too, like sediment, the very remnant of the old days. The report proved calming, because after the malicious gossip had spread like dust, after the palpable threat of scandal, after the worry surrounding the first inquiries, after predicting and believing the worst, there came an immense relief. Everything returned to normal; and that became a salvation since I was back to doing my duty before the Crown and my beloved lord, Don Carlos IV. All the shadows disappeared, not just those conjured up by malicious assumptions and the insidious report concerning the Queen herself as a result of her old rivalry with the Alba woman and concerning me since I had fought Cayetana for siding with the group rivaling me[1] (at that point, all scandal inevitably impregnated us), but also those shadows that covered, more secretly but with more dangerous proximity, another person eminent in the nation, whose link to a mysterious and strange death—let's not say premeditated murder yet—would plainly have constituted a tragedy for Spain's honor. But I believe I am getting ahead of myself in this story once again.

The order to inquire exhaustively into the causes of the Duchess's death had come from the King, Don Carlos, himself. I did nothing but carry it out, not leaving out, along the way, data that surfaced over the course of the investigation, some suggestions and recommendations, and I did not hesitate to make my own decision in the end: that of striking from the report an extreme suggestion that came up throughout during the questioning, because it would have been inconvenient and favorable for the propagation of new suspicion and rumors. Even though my diligence during the inquiries was paired with a censor's opportunity and zeal, all my efforts did nothing more than keep the Crown from a disturbance greater than the one the King had already been forced to confront. And the result was this relief, this returning the river to its banks, the professional and spare tone of this report against which, discouraged, the bad spirits of calumny and the bolder, if weaker, spirits of simple curiosity would be dashed and shattered. The case was officially closed.

But that did not preclude my conscience from being upset. On the contrary, I knew that the report was deliberately incomplete, that some essential data had, as if by sleight of hand, been made to disappear—and by me!—that its judgments were, if not bold or neglectful, then definitely the fruit of an adulteration. And that caused my feelings to be contradictory during the reading of the report: That relief and this uneasiness; that satisfaction of duty carried out before my lord; this knowledge of my part in making that blessed report a lie if only through omission.[2] Strange how, as I read that report so many years later on that restless night in Villa Campitelli, those same warring feelings were revived, as if once again it had been only a few days since Cayetana's death, as if my fears of hearing the discernible signs of her agony, audible around her palace, were submerged again by the suppurations of perverse imagination that again made "the old woman and her pet" (as the Queen and and I were cruelly nicknamed in the corridors and in some circles of the Puerta del Sol or the Paseo) out to be plotters of a criminal poisoning.[3] It was as if in gathering proof of our innocence, further suspicion that I myself and—horrors—even the Queen, could have been the murderers would arise again like a sinister jack-in-the-box. And the murderer so close, I imagined I could feel him breathing next to my bed . . . but, dear God! I was in Rome and it was 1824. Madrid and that twenty-third of July in 1802 were so far away in miles and in time. Still . . .

Damned Goya! What did he know! What had that uncouth peasant with beady, black witch's eyes guessed? What if his information or his imagination incriminated that same person, could he think that I was now going to receive his revelation gratefully and even with a certain vindictive pleasure?

The light was now coming through the jalousies. And as I was falling off to sleep, the thought of summoning Don Fancho to Rome began to appeal to me . . .

So, the next day, I changed the usual order of my morning stroll and started the day by going bright and early to the post office, where I sent a letter off to Bordeaux. This is what it said:

> My dear Don Francisco,
> Great was my happiness at receiving your news and knowing that you have your energies intact, always ready to compose new works of your genius and ready to undertake long journeys such as the one that just took you to France or that you propose to make

to Rome to visit me. Lamentably, although I have resided in Rome all these unfortunate years of exile, I have decided on a change of scenery. Although I still do not know if I will end up in London or Vienna (I rule out Paris for reasons that you may deduce), I will certainly begin the trip shortly.[4] But I will write to you again because, in truth, I would like to meet with you and talk of the past. While my Memoirs are still no more than a vague plan, at such time as I write them, if that time ever comes, I will only talk of political matters, things from which you, of course, were exempt.[5] Perhaps if we see each other, you could paint a portrait of me. By the drawing you sent me and which I appreciate so much, I certainly see that you have not lost your hand. The drawing is so interesting for the fantasy as well as for the skill of the sketch. On the other hand I, as you will understand if we see each other, have fully lost my bearing and vigor since for me these sad years have also gone by quickly.[6] I implore you to give my regards to Spanish friends with whom you may have dealings and give my love to the family members accompanying you. Is Javier with you?[7] With friendship and warm thoughts as always,

Don Manuel de Godoy
Prince of Peace

I kept a copy of the letter, as is my habit.

Notes

1. It may have been overlooked that, while the Duchess of Alba did side against the Queen and Godoy, with the

faction that had formed around Fernando, the young and controversial Prince of Asturias, she did so for a reason more viable than her old rivalry with the Queen. The other personality of that group was Minister Cornel, involved with the Duchess until 1800, but it is risky to conjecture that any lover could have such intellectual influence over her as to make her adopt some political party. What's more, it is unlikely that there had existed any true sympathy between two personalities so opposite—the one so vital and independent, the other so fainthearted and somber—as those of the Duchess and the future Fernando VII. One should consider that the Duchess, her looks fading, may simply have decided to dabble in politics, as any notable woman might have done in her position.

2. There will not be a shortage of people who will think that Godoy's guilty conscience is moved by a feeling akin to hypocrisy. But taking into account the way Godoy tried to portray himself years later in his Memoirs as having irreproachable honor, one must recognize the spirit of sincerity with which this eighty-year-old man gave this testimony.

3. We will argue further on that the use of poison had been so widespread in Europe since the Renaissance that attributing a murder by poisoning to a crowned head or to a governor was no more daring than supposing today that a head of state would order his secret service to use firearms to eliminate a politically dangerous person.

4. Godoy clearly lies to Goya. There was never more than a vague plan to settle down in England, discussed in his friendly correspondence with Lord Holland. Godoy seems to use the detail of "ruling out Paris" (doubtless because of the greater instability of the French government at the time) to make his lie seem more plausible. To the politically astute, capable of dodging the question until the very end, the entire letter reveals the truly compromising answer that Godoy

owed to Goya's offer "to relate vital details relative to a lamentable event."

5. In this last point, Godoy did do what he said he would. In his Memoirs he pays practically no attention to personal or private matters. This includes a reference to his marriage to the Countess of Chinchón, which relates exclusively to the political nature of that alliance. Pepita Tudó is not mentioned once, nor was his relationship with the Queen noted, except the glory that was hers. The vague mention of "calumnies and infamies"—never specified—attempts to cover it all.

6. When he wrote this letter, Godoy was fifty-seven years old. It is likely that idleness and frustrations had had ruinous effects, as he himself would insist later, on the physical vigor and good looks the ex-general-in-chief, ex-chief of staff once had.

7. Evidently, after so many years of having lost contact with Goya, Godoy prefers talking vaguely of "family members accompanying you," without any express reference to his companion Doña Leocadia Weiss or to that woman's children; he prefers to mention Javier, Goya's son. Presumably, Javier had been with his father since 1808, when Javier was twenty-four years old, and probably did not stay with him beyond his forties.

BORDEAUX, OCTOBER 1825

IN OCTOBER 1825, I decided to travel incognito to Paris with political motives that today I am not interested in describing.[1] So as not to arouse the Vatican chancellery's suspicion, I pretended to leave for Pisa as I did every month to visit the Countess of Castillofiel and her children, a habit that relied on tacit papal acquiescence; from Pisa, coach, horses, coachman, and postboy hired beforehand, I continued to Paris. There my affairs took a step quicker than I had foreseen—which, as they say in a good ballad, means they turned out badly or that I had envisioned things all out of proportion—and I decided to return to Pisa with no more delay, as much out of the desire to console myself with Pepita and my little ones,[2] as not to give an unnecessary edge of success to the Pontif's spies, considered the ablest in Italy, in their day.[3]

So, I took the road to Lyons, which would take me from there to Geneva and through Milan, to Tuscany. It was at an inn on the outskirts of Lyons, where one certainly dined splendidly,[4] that my eyes casually fell on a sign on the royal highway, a large, wooden arrow painted white with "BORDEAUX" written in bold, black capital letters. I do not know whether I was influenced by my agreeable digestion or rather by that very unfamiliar taste of failure that I was carrying inside me on my return to my maddening Italian seclusion. The fact remains that, forgetting those spies and my own desire for Pepita, I decided with no more pondering to turn off in the direction of Bordeaux. The horses were good ones, the coachman, able and jovial, and France is a treasure for the eyes in the fall, so I made the trip in good spirits. During the trip, I cannot remember to what degree my thoughts were or were not conjuring up the events that, inevitably, were going to be the subject of my interview with the old Maestro. I know that at some point I was struck by the fear that, over the course of a year, Goya could have died, and I would be left with my curiosity unsatisfied; but in that case, I decided, I would always be able to entertain myself with the freedoms of a Bordeaux exile, chat with people about Spain and the ever-so-much-more-remote prospects of returning to a government that was not as opposed to progress and as cruel as King Fernando's was, and one much more in keeping with our old dreams of a Spain synchronized with the clock of enlightened and modern history.[5]

I headed for Fossés de l'Intendance; curiously, its name has remained etched in my memory, because the painter's spelling—so picturesque in Spanish—turned out to be flawless in French, and that had amused me. But Goya was no longer living in that neighborhood; a helpful lady remembered her neighbor as a moody man *("tantôt gentil, tantôt farouche")* and his wife as a troublemaker *("une cancannière, une espagnole trop bavarde qui adore le raffut du ménage"),* but she did not know for certain if they were still living in Bordeaux or if they had moved to Plombières, which she had heard them discuss doing on more than one occasion.[6] My loquacious informant ended by finally telling me one important fact:

Goya, it seems, used to get together every day, "*l'après-midi,*" with other Spaniards at a chocolate shop owned by a fellow countryman named something like Poc. Or Pot. No, Poc. She was sure: Poc. Some of her young relatives used to sing a little sol-fa: "*Allons prendre un choc chez Poc, c'est le chic de notre époque.*" The chocolate shop was so popular among the people of Bordeaux themselves that it was not hard to find.[7]

I got directions that very afternoon at the inn where I was staying. I did not even need to take the coach. You could get to the "rue de Petit-Taupe" on foot in just a few minutes along a short and pleasant boulevard, with not many turns. On the way, crossing a plaza carpeted with dried leaves gilded by the midafternoon sun, I saw something in the vestibule of an inn that caught my attention: a poster announcing a production of *The Barber of Seville* that very evening, in the Grand Theater of the city. I was happy thinking that, if I did not find Goya, I could console myself with Maestro Rossini and above all with a visit to what was considered one of the most beautiful opera houses in Europe. We had even drawn up an imitation of it in Madrid, in a project to build a coliseum across from the Royal Palace.[8]

A little farther on (I still had not gone all the way around the plaza's main monument), I was surprised to hear Spanish being spoken. Two men were talking in very loud voices, the way we Spaniards talk in streets and taverns. I slowed my pace, so they would not notice me. Despite the time that had passed, I recognized one of them at once as that Bonapartist, Manuel Silvela; the coarse gravity of his voice and his knife-edge nose that the years had done nothing but accentuate were unmistakable.[9] Not so with the other man, whose decrepit features and defeated physique I did not identify right away as any old acquaintance. I slowed down a bit more, and I could see that they were taking the same route as I and, snaking down a narrow alleyway, they finally went into a shop called Maison Poc. But meanwhile something had happened. A kind of panic had come over me. I realized, with the speed and clarity of a lightning bolt, that I had so foolishly deluded myself to think that any encounter I would face with any of those refugee liberals in Bordeaux would be pleasant or beneficial. Although what they and I had each wanted for Spain a quarter of a century before was not so alien from the other, and our desires overlapped, we had fought in such opposite camps that it was foolish optimism to suppose that just the fact of being, like them, the victim of persecution by the same government was going to mean that they would welcome someone whom they had considered an enemy and his politics unlucky.[10]

In any case, I was not up to testing out that feeling, to exposing myself to rebuff or affront. I found myself two steps from the door of Maison Poc and probably from Goya, reluctant and groping for a way to put enough distance between those men and me. I was vacillating that way when my gaze fell on an old mirror that decorated the entrance next to the panel where you could read "*Chocolat et pâtisseries.*" The image the mirror returned to me, seen by my eyes caught off guard, was so different from the Godoy that these men had last seen nearly twenty years before. It was doubtful that they would recognize me! . . . My face looked hollowed and so very thin, my nose and mouth that long ago had been fleshy and sensual were sharp. Baldness was invading where soft hair once fell waving around my temples, my robust body was weakened and shrunken, the light in my eyes had dimmed as had the flush the Asturias wind had pressed on my skin. No one was going to recognize me. To pass unnoticed, I only had to put on my glasses, talk to the waiter in convincing French, and be discreet.

My entrance having provoked barely a few vaguely curious glances, I sat down a little out of the way, next to the window, to view in clear light the changes age had made, making recognition still more difficult. I identified Don Leandro de Moratín as the other man who had passed by my side, recognizing him to be hardly more than an echo, a repeat of my own fallen image in the mirror. Poor Moratín. He was a ruin of a man.[11]

They were not alone. Three more men were sitting at their table; I did not know them, although by their speech they were Spaniards. The five were talking in loud voices, joking with the man who seemed to be the owner of the chocolate shop (Poc?),[12] or making small talk, for all that their words reached me. They were certainly not conspirators; not once was the name of Spain even mentioned that I heard. One of them began to describe in detail a stupid bureaucratic foul-up in who-knows-what infernal office. And the tone of the conversation did not vary when Goya arrived.

Because Goya arrived a little while later, stopped for a moment in the shadows to catch his breath after negotiating the steep hole of a small mole—as the little side street was called. I was moved to see him after so many years, his stature and the look on his face still vigorous, although both were swollen over the years. He was by far the oldest man there, although he was certainly less affected by age. He had flourished, certainly, and he was the only one who surprised me, with his dove gray overcoat, his black leggings, and his pale cream jabot, a certain forced and conventional air, as if fifteen months in France had done more than thirty years in the Spanish Court could do to graft a uniform of bourgeois respectability on to the mixed stamp of farmer, bohemian, and dandy, which I remembered from Madrid.[13]

He sat down in front of me and two or three times, no more, he looked at me with eyes that still went through me, busy (as they always were) reading the lips of his cronies, although I doubt he could hear them. But those two or three times were enough to upset me. So, pretending to try to get the best light from the window on my newspaper, I changed places and sat with my back to him. I did not even dare to stay there for very long. The group promised to go on for a long time. It was unlikely that Goya would ever be alone so I could approach him. It would be better, in the morning, to leave him a message at the same chocolate shop, so he would be free to announce or not, at his discretion, my presence in Bordeaux to his friends. Then I left, thinking I was leaving as unnoticed as I had entered. I could not have said whether Poc's chocolate was excellent or terrible, I had been so wrapped up in the task of remaining incognito.

Alone in a box, watching a production of the *Barber of Seville,* thoughtlessly translated into French (*"Una voce poco fa,"* for example, was turned into *"Une voix ne trompe pas"*), the second act having begun, I noticed someone, a man, sitting in a chair near mine, settle into a prudent second row. I did not turn around or pay any attention to him. The contralto was beautiful and delightful, although she did not have the agility of a Malibrán.[14] But during the relentless applause that followed Don Basilio's aria (in which a *"venticello"* became a tortured *"une brise légère"*), the recent arrival put a knotted hand on my knee and whispered in a voice more resonant than the usual: "You like the opera, too, Highness?" Someone shushed us immediately. In the midst of my confusion, I managed, absorbed, to find myself face-to-face with old Goya who, not fully aware of the growing disapprobation of nearby spectators or waiting for my answer, added, knitting his brow over his astute eyes, "Above all to a painter, nothing reveals more about a person than the nape of his neck or the relationship between the head and the shoulders. I saw you this afternoon in Poc's place, and I guessed you were looking for me." He would have gone on talking perhaps in his out-of-tune, deaf man's voice, had not the shushing all around us doubled, had not the orchestra conductor given us a sharp glance as he poised in the air for the first stroke of his baton after the ovation, and had not I myself, uncomfortable as I had been feeling, imposed silence on him with a gesture perhaps too imperious.

Drinking champagne at the top of the stairway during the intermission, Goya had me admire the theater, its wide vestibule, its perfect proportions, the richness of the decorations, and above all the exquisite elegance of the graceful cupola that crowned the immense structure. "Do you remember, Highness?" he asked suddenly, turning to me, with a fixed look in his eyes, breathing heavily, his massive trunk leaning down from an upper step, "That night she showed off the palace and the galleries and the ceilings that I was going to paint for her and that grand stairway like this one. If time had allowed her, she would have built a cupola, too, because nothing intimidated her, right? She wanted to make her palace at Buenavista her monument in life . . . or her mausoleum . . . Poor dear." And abruptly, about to sigh, he contained himself, lowered his eyes, straightened his shoulders, drank down the rest of his champagne, and, in what seemed to me an attempt to hide his emotion, turned his back to me and went to set his glass down on a far table.

I had not brought up her name, but he had talked about her and about that night, as if there were no possibility of error, of a single misunderstanding, as if tacitly, from the minute he greeted me in the box, we two would not have thought about anything but Cayetana, her palace, and that funereal evening. And I asked myself whether, deaf as he was, he frequented the opera for any reason other than calling up images of other stairs, other friezes, other marble, and other mirrors.

So that, in the last act I did not manage to pay any attention to Fígaro's intrigues or to the sentimental avatars of Almaviva and his Rosina; to the beat of Monsieur Crescendo's melodies, the guests at Cayetana's last party danced in my imagination.[15]

Goya was now living on rue de la Croix Blanche, a more charming corner of Bordeaux: its trees with leaves still on them, its little houses tidy and unpretentious, its windows with tiny panes, its secluded gardens. A woman still young, more breezy than beautiful, with very dark and expressive eyes, dressed and coiffed with a lack of concern, came to open the door for me. "Welcome, Highness. I am Leocadia," she said impudently, immediately averting her eyes and extending her hand, but roughly pulling it away from mine, not giving me time to kiss it.

I had never seen her before. She must have been a teenager when I left Spain. All I knew of her was that she was a cousin of Goya's daughter-in-law and that she had been living with Goya for many years, along with some son of an abandoned husband. I was struck simultaneously by her vitality and shyness, but above all by her brusqueness that seemed to be the only bridge possible between the two traits, her way of talking so harshly, so quick and so much, her habit of hiding her apprehensive eyes and of fixing them abruptly on someone, as if it were a dare, a test, nearly a warning. She was clearly a woman who had gotten nothing in life free.[16]

Goya did not take long to appear, gotten up in the same outfit from the evening before, which seemed less tidy in the morning light. "Go on, bring us some coffee, Leocadia," he ordered the woman. "We have to talk," he added with a jerk of his head that puzzled me. That cutting, Muslim way of excluding women from men's business, even in the domestic setting, took me back to many years before. Away from Spain, I had begun to forget it.

The Maestro led me to a small, blue, glassed-in room that looked out on a garden, and which seemed to be—with its comfortable wicker chairs, its large bird cages, its books and magazines, and a table covered with a flowered, pale yellow cloth—a modest corner in which to enjoy the morning sun and perhaps to escape Leocadia's *raffut* and the *bavardage.*

She brought the coffee, made some comment that did not claim more answer than what she got—a smile from me and a grunt from the old man—and then left us alone. After his reference to the Duchess in the vestibule of the Grand Theater, we had not mentioned Cayetana again, and now he seemed to be resolving secretly which of the two was going to break the ice; without a doubt we were not thinking about anything else while we exchanged courteously superficial information about our respective exiles in Rome and Bordeaux. The conversation was not easy; it never had been easy with Goya since steadily, but at a progressively faster rate, he had been losing his hearing over the last thirty years. Now talking with him was even harder because he was completely deaf, and I had no practice whatsoever in the task of making myself understood by my lip movement or by some established system of gestures.

Luckily facing me, on the wall, was a nice sketch of a child playing with a little spaniel and I could study it closely, not because it really interested me, but to give myself a breather from the small talk. "That's a lovely sketch, isn't it?" asked Goya. And to my silent assent he added cheerfully. "Well, it isn't mine. Do you know who did it? Come over here." He motioned me over to the window, having me get to my feet, and he pointed to the garden. Four or five children were playing out there, their laughter and shouts rose up to us, muffled through the window panes. "The girl in blue," added Goya, "is our Rosarito. She did that sketch two years ago and now she's barely ten. I've never seen natural talent so extraordinary. Mme. Vigée-Lebrun will have little chance in the race for the title of first great woman painter in history."

He seemed overflowing with pride. Considering that pride and the girl's talent, I deduced that she was his own daughter. I never learned that for certain.[17] But I know that, over the years, she has not developed into what Goya dreamed of her being, although—and Pepita has written this to me from Madrid—she has taught drawing to the Queen of Spain herself.

With the pretext of showing me samples of the little girl's genius, he took me to his studio on the opposite side of the house. I did not hide my surprise. The sun bathing the room we had just left did not reach this part of the house, facing the north. "There's no more deceptive light for a painter than natural light," the old man explained. "I like painting at night. Or with the shutters closed."

The proof of that was before my eyes. The studio was full of candles, candlesticks, stubs of candles of all heights, tallow drippings on the wood tables and on the floor tiles, candelabras of all shapes and sizes, and I even saw, resting on a shelf, the famous, greasy hat, its brim spiked with thin, half-burned candles and globs of their wax and singed spots on its tall, discolored crown.[18]

We studied Rosarito's drawings and also some delightful miniatures on ivory with which Goya was experimenting with the enthusiasm of a young boy doing something for the first time, something that could open up for him who knows what horizons; and some etchings of bulls, done in technique called lithography, which, although it is hard to believe, was a new apprenticeship for this insatiable old man. It was no exaggeration when he insisted before in his letter: "I am still learning. . . ."[19]

At that point, I let my surprise show at not seeing any large painting or portrait in progress on the sawhorses, the way it used to be at his studio in Madrid. "This isn't the first time I've taken a long break from painting portraits," he said, suddenly somber. "For example, during the war, I didn't paint any portraits. How could I paint a gentleman at his study or a lady in her boudoir while people were being killed in the streets or on country roads?" And after a silence, he added, "And after she died, it was the same way. I went a whole year not painting a single thing." He raised his eyes to me, with a complicity I did not understand. "That is, with the exception of two portraits . . . Only two portraits that were tied to her death . . . " He walked away and began to clean a brush mechanically, distractedly. Finally he said, "We must talk about all this this afternoon, Don Manuel."

This time he had not addressed me as Your Highness. His tone had become more personal, almost bold. Suddenly, it was there, in the flesh, imminent, the promise or the threat from his letter. And the temptation that had brought me from Lyons, that had made me cross all of France. I was overcome, like a teenage boy who finally finds himself face-to-face with the woman of the street he has hired so eagerly, only to wish he were far away from her, with his parents. I faced Goya and enunciated my words with singular care.

"There was a police investigation at the time, Don Fancho. I personally ordered and oversaw it. The results were conclusive. There was no criminal hand in the Duchess's death. There was no poison." He understood me. A sad shadow passed over his face, a look of irony and disappointment. "You and I know that the investigation did not get to the bottom of things. To begin with, they didn't perform an autopsy. I know poison was involved. It is clear to me. I knew it beforehand. And I have proof." Everything around him had grown dark, as if in effect the shutters in the room had all been slammed shut, tight. Even his voice became dark and burning, with a vibration down deep, which seemed to send out waves you could actually see in the last syllable. "And you're writing your memoirs. You must know the truth."

I turned to face him, carefully enunciating every syllable of my comments. It was probably insensitive to get into a debate with him. "I haven't begun to write them. That's just a rumor. Perhaps I won't ever do it." He chose not to hear me. "I can't write. Nor can I paint what happened that day in a series of scenes, like those lives of saints that Carpaccio or Zurbarán painted. But I can describe them to you, almost minute by minute, and in some way dispel . . . " I interrupted him. I spoke with more energy, raising my voice, not concerning myself with his deafness. I told him that my memoirs, if I ever wrote them one day, would only tackle the political aspects of my government and of the reign of Carlos IV. For the first time he answered me as if he had heard me. "Then all the more reason, Don Manuel. The rumors that went around about a possible murder, didn't they point perhaps to the top? Let's say it outright. More than twenty years have gone by. Those two women have died. People accused the Queen. Don't tell me that all that did not have something to do with politics."

I was sorry I was there, as if I had, through clumsiness or candidness, gotten myself in a trap. I was not going to be able to talk normally with Goya. He would hear what he wanted to hear. The thought of arguing with him discouraged me. The mere mention of Doña María Luisa sounded like sacrilege to me. What was I to do? Then, with her usual brusqueness, Leocadia interrupted. "Fancho, lunch will be served soon. Are you hungry, Highness?"

During the meal, Goya could not hide his impatience. He alienated himself from all the conversation even at the cost of good manners, he barely ate and he drank more wine than Leocadia, he judged his surly comments to be prudent. Talking to Leocadia was not very comfortable, either. She insisted on calling me Your Highness every time she spoke to me, but that was accompanied by a familiar and petulant tone that belied that apparent respect, so that with my title tacked on, her frank tone lost freshness and came close to being a gross parody of great proportion, and with her bold, little tone, my title itself was ridiculed and devoid of feeling. It was a relief to see Goya stand up unexpectedly and to hear him say, "Don Manuel and I want to be left alone, now. You've talked enough already, Leocadia. Bring us more coffee in my studio. And a bottle of brandy."

Leocadia had saved me from Goya and Goya had saved me from Leocadia; but now I had no escape other than to leave. And hadn't I come expressly to hear what Goya, lighting the candles here and there, was preparing to tell me? Then, allowing time for Leocadia's last interruption, he set two chairs face-to-face and pulled the shutters closed. He waited for Leocadia to close the door, something she did with not a little force (I noticed that the vibration from the slamming door reached him but without its noise). He even waited for me to drink my coffee while he poured his first glass of brandy, having filled mine too quickly, even spilling some; as if an anxiety would consume him, make that steady hand tremble which, judging by his miniatures, still enjoyed perfect firmness.

Notes

1. There is no allusion in either Godoy's biography or in his Memoirs to this trip, to this far-fetched plan: A return to Spain? A plan for a coup d'état?

2. Notice how Godoy unconsciously shifts between hypocritical formality and confiding directness in the same paragraph, calling the same people "the Countess of Castillofiel and her sons" and "Pepita and my little ones." That pendulous swing between keeping up appearances and sincere confession is characteristic of this Brief Memoir.
3. Without meaning to, Godoy probably exaggerated the concern his movements could cause the papal chancellery and its secret service by 1825. Simply another delusion.
4. The gastronomical tradition of Lyons is legendary.
5. More expansively and with more insistence, Godoy is concerned in his Memoirs with appearing to be a *belle figure* with regard to his politico-cultural program at the end of the eighteenth century and the beginning of the nineteenth. In any case, one must recognize that his government was moderately enlightened; it incorporated in it a proportionately large number of the most prominent figures in philosophy and the sciences. Through those noted figures, it did much positive work. Certainly it did not persecute them the way Fernando VII did, with inquisitorial brutality.
6. Goya, as we have seen, went back to talking about Plombières and his water cure every time the moment arose to have his lawyer ask the King of Spain for an extension of his leave, but in reality he did not seem to have had any intention of going to take it, except for the vague references that the "helpful lady" reports.
7. That chocolate shop where the Spanish "intelligentsia" got together really did belong to an exile named Braulio Poc.
8. It was indeed copied, and with no false modesty, by Garnier in the Paris Opera.
9. Silvela was in fact living in Bordeaux in 1825 and had been since Joseph Bonaparte was ousted from the Spanish throne in 1813. He was only forty-four years old.

10. Godoy's foolish delusions concern all the contradictions that comprised Spanish ideologies during the reign of Carlos IV. At times, the same ideals of enlightenment and progress were shared by those battling in opposing political camps, contradictions that reached maximum tension between the Francophones, during the Napoleonic domination and the war of independence. But this topic goes beyond the aspirations of these notes.
11. Moratín was sixty-four years old in 1825. In December of that year, six weeks after the time Godoy saw him as "decrepit and defeated," he fell gravely ill. That illness gave him few moments of relief and carried him to his death in 1828.
12. Braulio Poc, as we have said, was Goya's countryman.
13. Godoy's acute observation gives us perhaps a valid interpretation of the portrait by Vicente López in 1826, which shows a bourgeois Goya, very different from his self-portraits. Until now, this difference has been attributed rather more to López's own perspective than to a transformation of his model, as Godoy proposes.
14. Godoy did admire Malibrán's art quite a while later, when he was already living in Paris, but he makes this retrospective comparison in 1848.
15. It is also the Godoy of 1848 who can talk of Monsieur Crescendo, a malicious nickname the French stuck Rossini with, at a very late stage in his career.
16. Leocadia Weiss was fifteen or sixteen years old when Goya met her in 1805, at the wedding of his son, Javier, to Gumersinda Goicoechea, Leocadia's cousin. Therefore, he was around thirty-five then. Her relationship with Goya, although we cannot say for sure, dates back more or less to 1813, when she leaves Weiss, her husband, once and for all.
17. Not just Godoy; no one has been able to determine with relative authority whether Rosarito Weiss was Goya's daughter or not, although Goya treated her as such and wanted her to be. Godoy is not wrong either

about the dark destiny of the woman artist or in saying that she was young Isabel II's teacher.

18. Goya was reported to wear a hat, like the one Godoy describes, when he painted the frescoes in San Antonio de la Florida. We can picture him, since we do not know for certain, dressed like this while he did the dark paintings at the Quinta del Sordo. Many years before in one of his many self-portraits, he immortalizes himself this way.

19. Goya critics agree with Godoy's affirmations. Except for part of the spring when he returned to recuperate from an illness (as in 1793 and in 1819), Goya probably dedicated himself in 1825 entirely to painting his miniatures and his bulls, later called "the Bordeaux work."

GOYA'S STORY

NOTICE TO THE READER

IT IS NOT going to be easy to describe my conversation with Goya that afternoon and to give a clear picture of those hours with him. He, in fact, carried on a monologue, giving me few chances to interject. From the start, I gave up trying to interrupt so I would not disturb the abundant flow of his memories with misguided exchanges between two men—one deaf and the other incapable of making himself understood. Of the many ways to face that difficult transcription, I have finally decided on trying to reproduce Goya's soliloquy, the way it flowed, its disorder, its emotion, and not pretend to imitate its fullness, picturesque quality, or even the bad Spanish he spoke. I have done such a thing successfully on the occasion of more than one verbal confrontation in my Memoirs. For example, I verbographically related my heated discussion with the Prince of Asturias in 1805, regarding a fact I told him about Nelson's armies. According to him I had reported that conversation deliberately in error. I was especially successful in relating the elegies as they had been recited to me by the renowned dramatic poet, Martínez de la Rosa. Those passages, according to de la Rosa, gave me a name for having natural talent for theatrical dialogue, at least in prose. That success has spurred me on to do it again. So that, even discounting that only in part will I carry my plan to a good port, and that my memory is inevitably subject to errors and alterations, including serious and always involuntary ones, here is the fruit of that ambitious undertaking. Of my role that afternoon, that of passive listener and receiver of Goya's extensive confidence, I will only point out, parenthetically, the most notable impressions I had during his discourse. Except for this moment, and excluding the parentheses, here then is Goya.

M.G.

GOYA'S STORY

I

WHERE DO I begin, Don Manuel? I don't want to go back to the past. I run the risk of getting caught up in it, and I wouldn't get to the part I want to tell you about. If you're interested . . . You are interested, aren't you? I'll take that silence for a yes. The past . . . I could really go back a long way. To the first time I saw her, in the Alameda de Osuna, at the center of a group of young people, organizing who knows what charity . . . She was playing cards, as usual. In those days, she was still very young. She had the deck of cards in her hand and was dealing them to a friend, like a gypsy . . . Have you seen those small paintings by that Dutchman Rembrandt, the light coming from who knows where, is centered on one person, inundating everything else with shadows? That's how it was with her. She was always dancing, laughing, dealing cards, or playing with her little poodle, and it was dark all around her. The light beamed down on her, and there it stayed, fixed, shimmering. I can picture her, any morning in Sanlúcar de Barrameda, that summer of 1796, splashing around in the pond with the little gypsy girl she'd taken in, two young girls, laughing, one dark, one pale, the same age, the same rank because of the joy of their nakedness and the cool water.

But as I've said already, I don't want to lose myself in the past. From that afternoon in the alameda and that morning in Sanlúcar until that sad month of July in 1802, I had known her, I had spent time with her, I had painted her . . .[1] What good does it do to go back over these things? If I don't begin there, I don't think I can sink my teeth in the story. You're a man of the world, Don Manuel. You knew about us, Don Manuel. I loved her. Everything revolves around that fact, like in blindman's buff. Don't we paint love as blind?

Years passed. The waters had calmed. I mean: I resigned myself. It was just a brief fling in her life. I! . . . who had wanted to be her one and only, and who committed that rash . . . or maybe I should say, innocent act of writing my name next to hers on two matching rings, on a portrait that then I couldn't let go of . . . as if it were the easiest thing in the world to do . . . you must have seen it. There was that signature at her feet, in the sand, "Only Goya," only me, my God, her one and only, how reckless, how pretentious of me! . . . And what a blow when I fell from that cloud. But all these years and years I've kept that portrait. What do you expect? I faced all of that, but the illusion still lived on, as if it could become flesh and blood, in those rings and that signature in the sand. And, she, poor thing, now must be nothing more than that . . . dust . . . sand . . .[2]

Years passed. Let's go to July 1802. By then we were nothing more than good friends. Not even a shadow remained—I don't just mean of love, but of the recriminations and the rancor. She had never understood very well—and I hadn't really tried to explain to her either—that I hadn't had any bad intentions in depicting her so often and so wrongly in my Caprichos; many times I injected more than a little irony, and, I confess, a touch of resentment. Maybe that was what had begun to drive her away. And I could never admit that to her face. We saw each other less. Her life had begun to change. You didn't see her at the theater, at the bullfights, at the galas anymore. Rumors spread that now she was wrapped up in politics and that she spent a lot of time at the court of the Prince of Asturias. She belonged to the party that opposed you and the Queen, right, Don Manuel? I'd never discussed government matters with her, nor had she ever seemed interested in them before. But, everyone talked about it; she was changing.

One day, I heard that she wanted to build a new residence, another mansion, and abandon that beautiful and beloved country house in Moncloa where years before I'd painted her, and erect an enormous structure in the gardens of Juan Hernández, taking away the people's park.[3] There was something strange about her. Strange how it meant nothing to her that she was offending the people of Madrid by giving full rein to a purely personal ambition. She had been so generous, so pure hearted, so indifferent to the temptations of grandeur. But she did it. Like a challenge. As if she'd said to the town: You love me; prove it. Put up with my whims.

One day, she summoned me to her new home. The garden was already fenced around with bars that kept the public out, but you could still hear the people shouting from the paseo, protesting the hated usurpation. Inside the vast mansion, surrounded by an army of architects, craftsmen, and laborers, she looked like a general getting ready for a lost battle, pale, high-strung, consumed by anxiety—I don't know if you can understand—as if her life depended on it. What little life remained to her. That afternoon, she showed me great halls and galleries, she showed me walls and ceilings and the grand staircase that we were reminded of yesterday in the theater, and she said to me, "Fancho, you must paint all this for me, walls and panels and ceilings and friezes and cornices; my palace must be the most splendid in all of Europe, greater than Empress Catherine's in St. Petersburg, and you will win immortality for having painted it!" Her eyes shone, her voice grew hoarse, she extended her arms like a sibyl; she was all fire in those days, but not with the ardor of youth. It was a tyrannical excitement, excessive, strident—allow me a simile from painting—a metallic color that filled me with fear because it wasn't like her . . . No one wants to admit the changes in people he loves. She had changed, and it hadn't been for the better.

After that meeting, I began to come to the mansion to study everything in it that I would paint, and, with her approval, I ended up setting up a small studio in one of the empty rooms. I put up frames and paintings; I built tables and easels. The treasurer, Don Antonio, allocated me all the canvases I wanted. I undertook the task. I did small, preliminary paintings in tempera according to the themes we had agreed upon. And here I got a surprise too. Expecting to please her, I began to sketch popular scenes, local characters, and doings of Madrid's street performers, the bullfighters and the dandies that she had enjoyed mingling with, but she didn't feel the same about those things either. And finally, to my regret, we agreed on episodes and heroes from mythology, and exchanged majas and flower girls for naiads and nymphs. And always looking for ways to make her happy, I began to dream up an immense and varied allegory in which a female protagonist—she, of course, although I held back the final surprise of painting in her face—appeared unrecognizable as a muse or nymph or goddess, until her final glorification on the ceiling of the great hall of mirrors, flanked by the four armies of Art, Thought, Poetry, and Love. My self-portrait, as if smuggled in, would be in one of the corners. And all the movement and rhythm of the piece would be that the gaze of the goddess would fall on it. It would be a secret prize that I, once more, would collect from immortality.[4]

All of this was no more than plans, a dozen sketches still vague and unrefined, when she announced to me, at the beginning of summer, that she was closing the mansion, suspending her projects, and taking off for Andalucía, despite warnings that an epidemic had broken out there and that it would be better for her not to expose herself in the heat of summer.[5] As I told you yesterday, Don Manuel, when she got something in her head, nothing would stop her. And so she took off, saying to me, "Fancho, while I'm away, don't paint—dream. I still don't like your sketches. You can see a mile away that it's a commissioned work. I want work that comes from your soul, that you paint in spite of me, where the genius of your painting shows up, the way it does in the dome of San Antonio." What could I do? I've always had little patience with any mythology that I hadn't made up myself. Maybe she would have accepted those witches and monsters of mine on the ceiling of her great hall![6]

(As he speaks, Goya tries to stay calm and poised, but doesn't manage to sit still in his chair. He gets up on any pretext, to light another candle or to retrieve the glass he has just left on a shelf or to fill mine, sometimes sitting back down on the footstool that faces his easel. And he sweats under his flannel jacket, his shaggy sideburns sweat, and the cream-colored shirt is soaked.)

On the afternoon of the twenty-second, I was working on that nude you'd hired me to do, Don Manuel. Remember? I never knew if you were serious or joking when you would say that my painting was going to have a prominent spot in your private gallery. Do you really have it? You're smiling. Never mind.[7] I was working on the nude, or I should say inventing a face for the lady, since at that point she didn't have one, going over sketches that I had found in my portfolio of some young girl. If your memory is good you'll recall that, when you arrived unexpectedly, I had the shutters drawn, like they are now, my hat on, the one you see over there with the candles on the brim, only they were lit. Okay, maybe it wasn't the same one, since not even the best felt can hold up under the tallow of so many years, any more than we can bear up under the big tears of disillusion life casts at us. Think about that comparison. You showed up then, to pressure me about the nude or to watch its progress. We argued about the face—you thought it was turning out too ordinary and I didn't; it had to be that way, I thought, that all the life of that painting should be in the tone of the body. The more neutral the face the better. You thought, or I thought you thought, that with the insignificance of the features what I was doing was erasing the identity of the nude body, because we two knew very well who it belonged to. We didn't need to say it, did we, Don Manuel?[8]

(What is Goya saying? That I knew that body or simply that I had guessed its owner's identity? I don't know. But I won't puzzle it out. I am the disinterested party here.)

The painting, of course, was a bold move. We two worried about guarding the secret—I, painting it in the solitude of my studio in the hottest part of the summer, when in Madrid people only visit each other at night; you, wanting it for a type of sanctuary where you would go, I imagine, with only your closest associates. But the events of history and of revolutionary politics turned Spain upside down like a beggar would a trash can. Someone ended up hooking our nude woman, the one we now call the maja, do you know that? And they didn't fish her out to admire her but to make her the scapegoat of the famous corruption of that time, and of your own corruption, Don Manuel, above all your own. You laugh! You didn't know that? You didn't know? It was back then, around 1814, when Don Fernando was already on the throne and the Holy Office had just been restored, in outright suit against you. Poking their noses in here and there, they dug up two majas, the nude one and the dressed one. They used them against me, too, since I had painted them for you, paintings that they were calling obscenities. Alongside Velázquez, Titian, Correggio, imagine the good company I was keeping. Those good inquisitors seized all those paintings, storing them in the General Depository of Sequesters, which had them in its power, and they dedicated themselves to studying them, or examining them, until they concluded that those paintings constituted a crime! A few months later, by May of the following year, it seems to me, they called me before the Holy Tribunal—if they could have, would have called Velázquez, Titian, Correggio, too. What a party that would have been—so I could identify the paintings and state that they were my work, when I painted them, who hired me, with what aim and to what end. Those are the exact words of the citation, I think, Don Manuel. Imagine, appearing before those holy gentlemen and saying that you had commissioned me to do them for your private gallery! So, I defended myself the best I could, like a cat on the logs. Things were getting rather nasty when, suddenly, the rumor began to spread that the woman in the nude painting was not just any model but a noblewoman. They invented many lies, but, curiously, the truth came out too. The name of the woman was on everyone's lips. Finally one of those canons who was questioning me, in a roundabout way, came up with her name . . . They didn't give me time to react. It was as if a flapping of black wings, as if an army of bats had invaded the audience room. The Inquisitor Tribunal adjourned the session. A week later dirt had been thrown on that fire, the investigation was reported to be closed, and they didn't bother me again about it after that. Someone had intervened; no doubt, someone highly placed, because as you well know that not even the King himself . . .[9] But I'm going out on a limb. Please try to forgive me. So many things have happened in Spain since you've been gone that you wouldn't grasp what little life is left for us to comment on.

So we were discussing, you and I, the nude's new face when Pedrín, that rascal, pockmarked boy who ran errands for me, came in to announce that the Duchess of Alba's coach had just stopped at my door alongside Your Highness's. I remember well the first reaction, yours and mine, was to hurry and put away the easel with the painting and cover it with a canvas. And I, I confess to you now, was asking myself at the same time, given my natural jealousy, if you two had agreed the morning before to meet at my studio. But if that were so, what possessed you to let her see the painting? And, then, why were you so anxious for me to hide it? . . . Foolish thoughts.

I didn't have much time to dwell on those thoughts. She had a quick step and was impatient on top of that. The linen cloth had barely fallen over the nude when there she was in front of us. "What a stroke of luck finding you in Fancho's studio," she said turning first to you. "They assured me that you were in La Granja. I had taken you off my guest list." I hung on her words always. Partly because of that singing voice, which rounded each vowel like a pearl, and partly because years before, she had learned to articulate for me, and she seemed to like stressing her lips' movement in a way that was so energetic and agile—and so seductive—the way she would have done if she were speaking French. "That's why I'm here, Fancho," she added. "To invite you to a party that I'm having tonight in honor of my cousin Manuelita, the little girl, remember her? Well, she's getting married to the Count of Haro. I want to celebrate her engagement, and I also want you to paint her. You will come? I can count on it? And you'll come, too, Manuel?" She turned toward you, and you exchanged some words I didn't understand, and I asked myself again whether you two hadn't made a date and if it wasn't all a trick played on a gullible person.

(It had not been. I suggest to him that perhaps on Cayetana's lips he did read the words she directed to me, and that today he prefers discreetly to ignore them. Cheekily she had said to me: "You will come, won't you, Manuel? Of course you will, I won't hear any excuses. This evening at ten, at my new palace; come in on Empress Street. You can come with any of your wives . . . " Goya turned red, choked, not denying or admitting that he heard her daring comment. And he continues his story determinedly.)

She walked to the center of the room, flung herself casually on the sofa in that way of hers, hands laced above her head, the way I'd painted her in the nude, all without taking off the mantilla that draped from the tall hair comb, shading her face. The veil cast shadows around her face; out of those shadows, her eyes shone like two blazing coals. She told us she had decided on the spur of the moment to leave Andalucía because she was bored. The epidemic was really a scourge. Her friends, frightened, had made up their minds not to stay there this summer. The town was gloomy and terrified, no one without some family member suffering. They had finally managed to get through to her and fill her with so much advice and so many omens that she'd come back to Madrid. To me that seemed a rather thoughtless and frivolous way to speak of that calamity, didn't it to you? Well, in fairness to her memory I should tell you, Don Manuel, I learned later that she hadn't left Andalucía without looking after her subjects who were down with the fever. She had taken a risk visiting them and caring for them. She had left them a large amount of money for medicine and vaccinations. It was just that, with her temperament, illness and death tried her patience more than anything . . . or maybe down deep she felt a premonition . . . "If you have finished, Manuel, leave us," she said finally, gathering herself up. "I have something private to discuss with Fancho, and I still have to work out the flower arrangements and take a look at all the preparations for tonight." You left right away. What special quality did that woman have that made obeying her as irresistible as ordering all other women around?

You hadn't been gone for more than a minute; all the while I was asking myself what she would want with me, she jumped to her feet and began to pace from one side of the studio to the other, with that walk only she had—long, lively, and swaying—that over the years was becoming more angular, more electric. Before I could stop her, she'd found the painting with the canvas thrown over it, peeked under the cloth, discovered it, standing face-to-face with herself nude. She choked on her words. "But this . . . " she began to say. She turned her back to me. I was expecting her to scold me, but there she stood, not moving, looking at the painting, until she turned around, her eyes shining even brighter from the shadow of her mantilla. "What's going on here, Fancho?" she asked. "Have you forgotten my face?" And as if her spirit were broken, she turned toward my stool and fell into a chair, pulled off the mantilla and exposed her face to the light, rigid, as if offering herself. "Well, you're in a fix, because that's why I'm here, to have you paint me." I was watching her, not registering that face that the years, too quickly, had ravaged. Finally I said carefully, "Another portrait?" She laughed bitterly. "Fool. What I want," she explained, "is for you to paint right on my face, with your paints. These days even with makeup I can't manage to improve on this desolation. Tonight I'm giving a party, and I don't want Manuelita's fifteen years or the bitch from Osuna to outshine me."[10] Now it was clear, sadly clear, what she was asking me to do, and despite my protests she begged and begged me until I had no other choice but to agree. She dried her tears. It wasn't rare for tears to fall suddenly from her eyes, like, in spite of herself, floods from a heart that was overflowing its banks. "Remember?" she said finally, "If you can remember my body so well," and she pointed to the nude, "it won't be very hard to give me back my face." I protested again, already beaten, said something gallant that I'm afraid must have sounded hollow, because the truth is that for three or four years she had been noticeably losing her marvelous vigor. Her skin was becoming wan, losing the color and bloom I remembered, her eyes were too feverish and even a little swollen, even her beautiful, beautiful hair seemed to be thinning and losing its shine. As if something were consuming her from inside, an illness . . .

(Goya isn't exaggerating. Two years before, at least, I remember. Cornel was minister at that time, and Cayetana had gone with him to dine with the King and Queen. Doña María Luisa had described her to me as "a wreck." I had thought that it was a judgment clouded by jealousy. But a few days later I ran into her—I hadn't seen her in a long time—at a party at the Alameda de los Benavente-Osuna; the untimely decline of that beautiful creature truly alarmed me.)[11]

An illness, Don Manuel . . . And I thought I knew what it was, although I didn't dare talk about it with her; I had no proof; I couldn't mention it. Around 1796, during the years we were the closest, the time we were together in Sanlúcar, she returned one night very excited from who knows what party she had gone to and told me that she had discovered a wonderful medicine. Someone had brought it from America in its raw state: leaves from a bush; the Indians in the altiplano of the Andes chew it. You have probably heard people talk about it. I'd heard about it and its extraordinary effects, too, at Court. And someone had come up with a process for steeping or distilling or synthesizing it . . . an alchemistic process, believe me, witchcraft . . . which produced a fine powder that you just had to inhale through your nose for it to start to work on your nature.[12] She opened up a beautiful little snuff box filled with that powder they'd just given her, and which she liked from the very first. Truthfully: We both tried it that night . . . and many nights during that time. I began to be enthusiastic, because for a while I thought the powder worked on the senses and on the brain in a way that seemed to double other perceptions. My understanding of color and form, real or imagined, would seem doubled, and I would finally become the painter I always dreamed of being, able to paint something that was beyond the superficiality of everyday life, the world of our fantasies and of our dreams! But the price was too high. I understood it in time. Remember a Capricho called *Volaverunt?* The maja very proudly wears a large butterfly on her forehead; it seems to drag her in flight toward some region of delights, and she doesn't pay attention to the monsters crowded around at her feet, waiting to ambush her. But the monsters win out in the end; do you understand what I'm saying? And the butterfly is nothing more than a mirage. This terrible dust fills our head with wonderful rainbow butterflies, but in the end it plunges us into the gray horror of the demons. This is the point of *Volaverunt.* As I said before, I understood in time. You get a habit, you begin to need the medicine more and more often, and you end up becoming its slave. I shared my fears with her. She laughed. She blamed my suspicious, peasant spirit, the narrow-mindedness of my age. Soon our relationship ended in a rupture—no, I don't mean that the famous little dust had any influence whatsoever on that. I returned to Madrid, defeated and bitter; she stayed in Sanlúcar, surrounded by a small court of bullfighters who, if my suspicions are not wrong, had become initiated in the same habits. And so, as love or jealousy changed later on into a forbidden theme between us, neither did we ever talk of that (the powder, that is) again, as if deep down, in an unconfessable way the subjects were mixed. And then many years later, I saw her seated in my study, so docile, so lifeless, ready for me to paint her like a canvas, like a panel, like a piece of copper. I didn't dare say to her: It's that damned powder. I'm sure, you went on taking it, and it has destroyed you. Stop taking it, there's still time, stop taking it, and you'll be beautiful again like yesterday, and you won't have to submit to this humiliation, my returning beauty to you with my art, a light, and a color that were yours, only yours . . .

(Goya continues putting such passion in his story that, in the middle of this afternoon, all that happened that afternoon in July 1802 seems recent once more, and with what you could call its magic effect, Goya is getting younger, getting his full and virile voice back, an ardor in his little eyes, a spring in his step. He even begins to seem more like the Goya of my first memories rather than the man I saw twenty-four hours ago in Poc's chocolate shop.)

But I didn't say anything to her. I collected my smallest brushes and a full pallet of colors on a little table and began my work, using not only my artistry but what I had learned watching my actress friends, especially La Tirana and Rita Luna, molding their faces delicately and astutely with makeup before they posed for my portraits.[13] For a painter it wasn't hard to recall those techniques: ochers as a base, various crimsons on the cheekbones and temples, blacks ringing the eyes, shades of pale ochers, greens, and purples in the hollow of the brows and in the eyelids. You can imagine how I felt, my fingers smeared with paint like a young girl's or a hairdresser's, coloring that face that, devastated as it was, was hers, the woman I had loved, that who knows, even then . . . Enough of that. I shouldn't dwell on that subject. I am incurable. At seventy-nine, I'm still incurable. Well, little by little, her complexion's vigor, the youthful glow, the soft shades of her coloring, the velvet look were coming back; in the final effect, all artificial, but exemplary. I considered my work finished; anxious and overbearing, she demanded a mirror. I ran to get her one. I wanted her to be what she was before. That had been too much for me. I don't know which of us was more humiliated. I starting putting my brushes away.

She said something about her neck. I wasn't looking at her. I barely heard what she said and was too upset to pay attention to her. But when I had put away my brushes and turned toward her, I saw her, holding the mirror above her chin, painting her neck white with her fingers, which slid lightly but nervously under her chin. It took a moment for what she was doing to sink in, and suddenly I leaped toward her, shouting, grabbing the white paint from her hand. Flinging her on the sofa, I began to scrub her neck with my own cravat, in desperation. It took a moment for her to grasp what was going on—you also, Don Manuel, ask me with your eyes, eh?—I finally got through to her with one word in the midst of her shouts and protests and kicking: Poison! Yes, poison! The silver white is poison, a very dangerous poison, and I had been very careful not to use it, it and other paints equally noxious, as the makeup with which I painted something as delicate as a woman's face.[14] We finally calmed down; and I toned down my reproaches and she, her complaints and jeers; I worked very hard to get every bit of the white off her. Even though she complained of the sting, at least I had avoided a poisoning.

"Too bad," she lamented, "I see I'll have to wear a scarf around my neck tonight, what all old women resort to." And she marveled that the materials that we painters use could be so harmful; I had to tell her about the cobalt violet and the Naples yellow and the Veronese green ...[15] "It's a trick," she commented. "They have the most delicious and poetic names and they can be as lethal as cyanide or arsenic . . . " She jumped to her feet again. This time I hoped she would leave, but she dashed those hopes: She started walking around my studio again, stopping in front of the nude, commenting to herself so I couldn't hear her, and prying among the covers, here and there, up and down, even taking things from my containers. She finally found what she was looking for: the last portrait I did of her, the one in Sanlúcar, the one she used to call her "portrait in black." And she didn't stop until she made me lean it, two meters or more high, against the back of a chair. There she was, as if in front of a mirror, a woman seeing herself in the other, the two painted by me, but the irony was that the woman in the painting now had a more authentic beauty and youth and seemed to say: "This is who you were." And almost like an echo of my thoughts, I hear her actually say: "That's how I used to look." And she runs toward the nude and points to it with an accusing finger and adds: "Like that . . . " Resentful, disheartened, she turns toward me, as if my paintings represented an offense graver than memory itself, and she warns: "One day I'll come here to have you paint my body, Fancho, and I'll make you paint me all over with that mercury, like painting a shroud. That's how I'll die, like that."

She seemed defeated. That bravado and ardent temperament of hers had left her, as if she had figured things out, life itself, and the struggle it involves, that it wasn't worth the price—and she went back to studying her "portrait in black," calm, silent, like an industrious little girl studying in front of a blackboard. This time she didn't have any comment on the "Goya" of the ring or on the "Only Goya" in the sand that she is pointing to in her portrait. She never did. I suppose it was her way, to disagree in silence. But at the same time she refrained from protesting. I imagine that reaction was none other than respect from a woman overly sensitive and tender toward love that had been awakened without anyone planning it. Then she came toward me, took me by my hand and had me sit down next to her, on the sofa. Not letting my hand go, she said sadly, "Thank you, Fancho, for having preserved me young and beautiful forever, and with a will to live, in your portraits of me, in your drawings, in that nude that I would want to have my face, so that everyone will know I was like that. These days I don't think about anything but dying or disappearing, keeping the spectacle of my decline from myself and from everyone. You have helped me live," and she pointed to the place where her portraits were kept, "just as you could help me die, letting me come back one day to your paints and . . . Don't interrupt me! Don't tell me that wouldn't be right! What did the dispirited woman die of? Of Naples yellow! It's better to die of mere yellow fever; that is the fashion of the times." She laughed, cried, I don't know which. I was very afraid. Suddenly she brushed a tear from the very tip of her eyelashes. "I'd better not cry," she said. "Your brave work would go to the devil." And she grabbed up her mantilla and left, but this time very carefully, like someone leaving a room with a sleeping child. What she was leaving, cradled between us two, was the idea of her death.

(Goya pours himself another glass of brandy. This time he forgets to fill mine. He has taken off his jacket and untied his cravat. His hair, damp with sweat, looks dark. Despite the terrible melancholy of his story, telling it rejuvenates him; he recovers the look of the Goya of 1802. You only need a little imagination to see Cayetana by his side, full of the gratitude and affection she had found for that small, robust dark-haired man who sweats from unbreakable fidelity.)

Notes

1. That afternoon in the alameda could very well date back to 1785, the date on which Goya paints his first two portraits of the Benavente-Osunas; Cayetana de Alba was then twenty-three years old. Ten years later, just after being appointed director of the Academy of San Fernando (the Duchess's mother unavoidably boasted of the honorary presidency of that organization), Goya got a visit from the Duke and Duchess of Alba. They commissioned him to paint a portrait of the two, which he did. After that he begins to see the Duchess, who is widowed at the end of that same year. Later, in 1796 and 1797, the relationship between the painter and his model-friend-patron-lover reaches its peak. And of their sojourn together in Sanlúcar de Barrameda, there remains the marvelous testimony of his album of drawings. The Duchess appears in one of them, just as Goya says, playing with her little gypsy friend.
2. The portrait Goya refers to somewhat incoherently is the most famous of those he painted of the Duchess, in which she appears in a black dress and mantilla, pointing at the ground. It was actually in the hands of the painter (against all logic) when his wife, Josefa Bayeu, died in 1812. Upon making an inventory of his goods by a notary's act, he already had entrusted it to his son, Javier. It is listed as "a portrait of the Alba woman with the number 14 (estimate) at 400 (reales)."
3. The gardens of Juan Hernández were open to the people of Madrid, who had made it into one of their favorite places to relax, until the Duchess, recovering old

ownership rights, decided to take it back and build her palace of Buenavista on it. Her action was enormously unpopular, and one could understand how even a person so beloved the way the Duchess was by the people of Madrid would suddenly see her name reviled in posters, which neither the Inquisition nor the King could keep from being displayed. Godoy, fallen as he was, got City Hall to agree upon the death of the Duchess that he be allowed to buy Buenavista for himself. After that the palace was by turns the Military Museum, the residence of the regent (1840), the Turkish embassy, headquarters for the artillery, and finally, the Ministry of War.

4. Nothing remains of Goya's studies for the murals and ceilings of the palace. Unhappy with the themes and execution, stricken by the death of the Duchess, whom they were meant to glorify, he may have had them destroyed.

5. While history has concerned itself more with the epidemic of yellow fever of 1803, which was a catastrophe throughout all of Andalucía (Godoy himself dedicates a great deal of his Memoirs to describing it and to reporting the number of doctors employed to combat it), there was an outbreak nearly every summer. As we see, the one in 1802 was not insignificant.

6. The disinclination for mythology that Goya confesses is true. Except for four or five of his first works, dating from his apprenticeship in Italy, there is no mythology in any of Goya's paintings, other than the very personal one of his Caprichos and Disparates—and that at the height of neoclassicism.

7. One of the more commonly held theories concerning the execution of the majas is confirmed here: They were painted under Godoy's commission, in whose possession they were found when his belongings were confiscated in 1808. As far as the private gallery that seems to have existed—in 1802 it may have been no more than a project—at least in the Buenavista Palace, it included, in

addition to the majas, nothing less than the *Toilet of Venus* by Velázquez, *Mercury Instructing Cupid* by Correggio, and the *Bacchae* by Titian, acquired by the Prince of Peace from the Duchess's heirs.

8. Here, Goya gives us a very simple explanation—simple for the painter—for the problem (namely the maja's neutral expression) that has so perplexed critics.

9. Except for notice of the citation—the text of which Goya recites from memory with notable accuracy—all sign of the case against Goya, including his acquittal, has disappeared completely from the archives of the Inquisition. Another inquisition, apparently, was interested in making it disappear. A new case of silence regarding the life and miracles of the praiseworthy Cayetana.

10. Finally there is a precise date for the celebrated letter from Goya to Zapater, which commentators used to date sometime between 1795 and 1800, and in which Goya says to his Zaragozan friend, "It was more worth your time for me to come to you to paint the Alba woman than to put her in my study so that you could paint the face on it and be done with it . . . " The letter has to have been written on the morning of the twenty-third, when Goya still did not know that "the Alba woman" was suffering in her palace.

11. The letter from the Queen exists and has been published. In the text of it, Doña María Luisa says: "The Alba woman came to say good-bye this afternoon; she dined with Cornel and left. She has become a wreck. I definitely believe that what happened to you before wouldn't happen to you again; also I believe you will be repentant of it." The allusion to an old amorous *affaire* between Godoy and "the Alba woman" is very clear.

12. Interest in the American plants, with their strange medicinal properties, was so great in Spain at that time that a year did not go by without new volumes being published on the "Peruvian Flower" by Don Hipólito Ruíz and Don José Pavón. Godoy himself says in volume

one of his Memoirs: "In those years we got new shipments from Peru for the increased use of the Peruvian and Chilean Flower that our botanist Juan Tafalla sent to us, more than one hundred new species, an increase not only for the luxury of science, but also for medicine, because of the strange virtues of some of the plants, roots, and bark that they have sent us." It is not at all strange that one of those plants "of strange virtues" had fallen into the Duchess's hands.

13. Goya did paint La Tirana on two occasions, in 1794 and in 1799, but he did not paint Rita Luna until 1814; that we know to be true. Either there is an earlier portrait of the actress that has disappeared or Goya had a lapse of memory, or Godoy put the reference in, recalling Goya's words. La Tirana and Rita Luna were celebrated actresses of their day. It makes sense for Goya to bring them up in the very strange, critical moment when he "makes up" the Duchess.

14. The silver white, also called lead white and Krems white (a basic carbonate of lead), was practically the only white used by the artists until the middle of the nineteenth century and figures among the most toxic of paints regularly used by them. It produces an illness dramatically called saturnism. The Brazilian painter Portinari died of poisoning by silver white. Nevertheless, in this case Goya's concern was excessive because, while he is right to recommend emphatically not breathing it or swallowing it, the toxic effect is the result of the accumulation of many small quantities. Anyway, Goya was not the only one to exaggerate its dangers; it was always considered toxic. Great precautions were always taken in its use.

15. The cobalt violet is arsenate of cobalt and should be used with extreme prudence; the Naples yellow, antimonate of lead, poisonous like all the colors made of lead; and the so-called Veronese green (in France), opaque green (in Spain), emerald green (in England), schwein-

furt (in Germany), is a combination of arsenic and copper acetate. More poisonous and dangerous than all the colors, it is given the most fantastic names to set it apart. (The Scheel green, used long ago, was pure arsenic, pure poison. One cannot rule out that Goya used it under another name, one given to a similar green.) It is no surprise that Goya would call it Veronese green. Aside from the fact that he could have learned to call it that in Italy, a Venetian, Tiepolo, had a great influence on Spanish painting during the second half of the eighteenth century, and Goya was not exempt from that influence. Tiepolo could well have attached the name "Veronese" to a green that he had picked up from the Maestro Paolo.

GOYA'S STORY
II

I arrived at the party too early, as usual; she still hadn't come down from her rooms. So, I chatted with members of her household: Don Ramón, the chaplain; Berganza, the secretary; and Sr. Bargas, her treasurer,[16] all were used to being around at the beginning of all her parties; then, as soon as the guests took over the terrain, they slipped away discreetly. We were tied, they and I, by an old friendship, and that night their concern, which I was obliged to share, was about a serious threat of fire in the palace a few days before. Everyone assumed it was intentional; the people resented what they considered an encroachment, still so vivid that not even the royal decree recognizing the Duchess's rights to the property could appease them.[17] What those faithful servants, the emotional Berganza especially, feared was a direct attack against their mistress and the way such an attack would affect her spirit—which already seemed to them uncharacteristically upset and apprehensive since her return from Andalucía. But as if flatly denying those worries, she appeared in the hall, giving her final orders and putting the finishing touches on the flower arrangement that she found in her path, showing no signs of the melancholy that distressed her secretary and the others, and that had concerned me in my studio a few hours before. She looked like the woman of her glory days. Secretly I felt proud to have contributed to that. She had done herself up skillfully, outfitted in a filmy dress of muslin in golds and flames, with layers and more layers on top of those, creating the look of a sunflower, with rubies and gold clustered at her neck, on her ears, and on her fingers to repeat her image in their sparkle. She was resplendent and she knew it. She turned to me and grabbed my hands, drawing me to the side. "See, Fancho, my dear," she said to me, "I've stayed away from all the poisonous colors. And I really wanted to wear my silver and white dress tonight." Saying that, she moved away to straighten the flower arrangement in a large porcelain vase. All the roses brightening up the decorations repeated the colors of her finery, like a variation of the same musical theme! But meanwhile, I tried to figure out if I should take those ambiguous words of her literally, or if they held some secret message about the silver white and her fantasies of death that we'd talked about that afternoon. In any case, she had upset me again, driving away the happy image her entrance had produced in me. Just then, the guests began to arrive.

No one had that natural grace and those fine arts of hospitality that she had, that let her dare to mix people of the most diverse classes in one parlor, theater box, or side by side at a dinner table. No one challenged that scepter, right? And in her house you knew you could find a bullfighter chatting with a grandee of Spain and a wise philosopher holding court with an actress. Always for the greater pleasure of everyone, because the free and relaxed atmosphere came from the hostess herself. You must remember that. She didn't shrink from involving a prince of royal blood and a man of the street in the same gathering, an aristocrat and a maja from Lavapiés in the same merriment. Happily, if she was changing, you didn't see her losing her flexibility. That night the guests began to arrive and after a while, as if on cue, the Prince of Asturias himself got together with Isidoro Máiquez and Rita Luna, and the bullfighter Costillares with the Count-Duke and Duchess of Benavente-Osuna.[18] I don't know just when you arrived, Don Manuel, but I do remember your being there, talking animatedly, even though just the presence of your political enemies—the Prince of course was an enemy, but so was Cornel, right? and even the mistress of the house herself—could get your dander up with the least provocation. She had that talent and that hadn't faded. You must have noticed her talent that night, Don Manuel. Well, you saw her, divorced from all your nostalgic memories, dark black eyes of hers lit up by the bright glow of her muslin dress. Around her, everything became a joy of living.

(Cayetana's talents being what they were, the beginning of that party was not as harmonious as Goya wants to remember. But he dodges it out of delicacy, it would seem, having alluded to an incident that took place in that first hour, and which caught all of us off guard. By then, I had been at the party for some time with Pepita, when my wife made her entrance accompanied by her brother, Luis, the Cardinal. Neither Mayte nor I had expected to run into each other there; she didn't even know that I had arrived from La Granja that very day. Running into each other was a blow to us both and resulted in the embarrassment of Cayetana and everyone who noticed our surprise. I mention it to Goya and he admits having noticed it.)[19]

I have no reason to deny it; I picked something up in the air. For a deaf man, who happens to be a painter besides, or if you prefer, for a painter who has the disgrace of being deaf, there is a way of listening . . . with your eyes, I mean, to replace the clues that come to us through our hearing. I remember that moment clearly. Doña Pepita, who was standing next to me, suddenly closed her fan, which trembled in her clenched fist. I turned and saw the Cardinal's hand hesitate, wavering in the air, longer than he needed to, as he extended it toward the hostess who was bending over to kiss his ring; I saw the fleeting surprise replace the weak smile on Mayte's—sorry, the Countess's—lips. Forgive me; remember, I'd known her since she was very young.[20] And I also saw you come forward to greet her a bit quicker and with less aplomb than would have been natural; I saw a flash of malicious joy in Don Fernando's bulging eyes; I noticed a tension, the way those figures froze, which I imagine were covered up by the living and uninvolved figures of their doubles that were crossing there; but above all I noticed, returning to Cayetana's side, her black eyes still disconcerted, annoyed and amused by the surprise, and her cheeks had another blush of life on top of what my crimsons had put there. A while later she explained to me, laughing, that the whole incident had been a misunderstanding; I don't know if she got around to explaining it to you too. The Cardinal had been invited because he was a friend of the Count of Haro and because he was going to conduct the Count's wedding. He had announced that he would attend with his sister; she thought that he had meant his sister-in-law, Doña Luisita, not your wife. And she had even forgotten that when she had run into you at my studio and invited you to the party.[21] I can only tell you that she did not attach a lot of importance to those errors of ceremony or to those thorny key moments of mundane behavior. She was laughing with her cousin Pignatelli when I found her in the dining room, changing the place cards to sweeten the bad taste in everyone's mouth—your wife, you, Doña Pepita, and even the Cardinal. "I would have liked to have seen Berganza's face!" she said—Berganza was her secretary, a man overly concerned with etiquette. And still laughing, we went into the hall where the guests of honor, the engaged couple, the Count of Haro and the petite and delightful Manuelita, had already gone.[22]

The bad moment had passed. And she went on chatting till dinnertime in excellent humor. But Don Manuel, if you could have seen, as I did, my compelling need to polish my powers of observation and make my sight double—careful, don't smile, I don't intend a double meaning—you would have noticed how I compensated my wisdom and yet would have been able to read in my actions what was happening to me in turn. I don't know, you might have read it in the way I went over to stand by the windows for example, pretending to look at the garden. Because the truth is that while she had that admirable talent for bringing together the most unmatched people, she also had a damnable mania for surrounding herself with all her old lovers and admirers. That night, I won't say that they were all there, but I'm sure that they made up a damnably large percentage of her guests. And with all of them except me, I at least felt I was to blame for my old, pig-headed jealousies, she flirted, as if stirring up the embers: with Pignatelli, who came and went as he pleased at the palace since he was her cousin; with Cornel, who continued to conspire with her in Don Fernando's chambers and who hadn't stopped seeing her; even with Costillares, who had ardently taken the side of the wronged townspeople and who had courageously fought her plans to build the palace . . . For all of them she had a whisper, a secret laugh, an intimate tap of her fan on their chest at their heart, an impulsive touch of her hands lingering too long, and the worst of all, a tear, that ready tear, that bloomed in her eyes but never quite spilled over, and which fleeting, like lightning, was aimed at the heart, too. That worry made me twice deaf. Never had those lips seemed more subtle and insinuating to me as she was saying those incomprehensible and possibly innocent phrases; directed to others, they seemed to me to be charged with sensuality and mystery. And so I stood, deaf and jealous, studying my little snuff box when the dinner hour arrived.

(Goya seems younger than ever when he revives his jealousies; maybe he is holding back because no doubt those jealousies are rising against me, and he—with the perception of those jealousies and his own vision, which he has demonstrated was notable—couldn't have overlooked that I was, like Cornel, Costillares, Pignatelli, and himself, one more lover in the chorus of Cayetana's long-ago last party.)[23]

We were seated one facing the other, across the center of the large oval table. She had left the two places at the head of the table for our young guests of honor as an excuse, I suspect, for seating the guests who bored her the farthest from herself: Prince Fernando and the Count-Duke of Osuna, who in passing she was honoring by putting them to the right of the Count of Haro and the young future Countess. She sat, amused, between two gentlemen of greatly different temperament and pomp, the Cardinal and Costillares. With the first I know she liked to talk about gardening, one of her late passions; with the bullfighter she always maintained a very lively and aggressive relationship, which to my fears still smelled of a half-put-out fire. As for me, my dining partners were Rita Luna, who was very easy for me to talk to because she had an actress's precise diction, and the Countess-Duchess, who announced to me, making a noticeable effort to articulate with her extremely thin lips over her enormous teeth, that she wished to hire me for a new series of small panels for her new parlor, since she knew I was less than absorbed by my work as First Painter to the King.[24] But the individual conversations—not only my own, which were necessarily limited, of course—quickly took a back seat to a subject that caught everyone's attention. Someone mentioned the matter of the failed attempt to set the palace on fire. Questions, explanations, conjectures, jokes were tossed back and forth. I didn't pay much attention to them until the bantering finally ended, so that our hostess could inject her opinion or her own theory. She didn't get carried away with the subject, guiding the discussion instead to jokes and absurd theories. Still, I knew her too well not to detect, in her uneasy glance and in her gestures, how deeply the episode had really affected her, more than she was ready to admit. To think that anonymous hands would be so moved by resentment toward her as to try to destroy her longed-for palace. But, as I say, she chose to go the route of jest. And after teasing Costillares, whom she accused laughingly of having put the arsonists up to it since he had set himself up as the "champion of the common folk," she went down the length of the oval table sniffing out other possible enemies. She joked with you, Don Manuel, about the rancor you must have felt toward her since she had been part of that band of your political rivals. She joked with the Countess-Duchess since they were longtime rivals in matters of patronage of actors, bullfighters, and poets. And suddenly, she came face-to-face with me and just moving her lips, I'm sure, said to me: "You don't need fire from torches, Fancho; you have your violets and your greens to do away with me, but you won't do that till I ask you, right?" And I was very upset, not knowing if everyone else had heard or understood her words, and trying to figure out what kind of joke or what kind of truth there was in those words of hers. From that moment on, I chose to draw into myself, and I didn't try to hear anything the rest of the meal. I watched her, moving from one side to another, gesturing and laughing, and I asked myself over and over why she had that stupid obsession with poisons.

(I don't want to tell Don Fancho, but the obsession with poisons, at that point, almost seems more his than Cayetana's. I didn't hear Cayetana's remark, if she said it, and in any case it was in passing, in the middle of a conversation that had certainly been embarrassing and extremely bold, in which Cayetana had played dangerously with the truth, as she was fond of doing: her political animosity toward me, her plotting with Fernando, Escóiquiz and Cornel, her own rivalry with the Queen. The Prince himself, always up to something devious, never missed a chance to bring up that rivalry to upset everyone. But Goya, obsessed by the matter of the poisons, had noted none of those tensions, despite his sharp powers of perception. However, I now surmise that Cayetana's casual phrase, which I didn't catch, was certainly heard and registered by someone seated at that table who was by then ready to consider mortal poison.)[25]

She had received her guests, and we had dined on the first floor in some of those rooms that had been furnished provisionally and later were planned only to be offices for the owner of the house, her secretary, and treasurer; besides that, only the chapel and the vestry were finished. But with dinner over, she said she intended to show us around the entire palace, unfinished and unadorned as it was; she didn't wait for anyone's consent: An army of servants was already at the foot of the grand stairway, armed with tall candles, ready to light the way. And so began that strange night walk by torch light, everyone in a haphazard line going up the steps of that magnificent stairway, one of the spaces I saw that needed to be properly decorated, even though I was just going to have to compete with the richness of the marbles and golds. She was explaining all this as we climbed up the stairs, so anxious to tell her guests everything, her servants lighting it all up on cue as she pointed it out while our shadows grew ghostly, toward the highest ceilings, and the conversation that I picked up through the vibration of the air became effervescent with exclamations in the great emptiness. We followed after her, through the glass corridor around the patio—the reflection of the flames in the glass made the procession even more fantastic—to the small octagonal parlor that opened, through one of its walls on to the great hall of mirrors, the room that one day would be crowned by my allegory. There, in the middle of a tight rectangle of servants, whose torches were multiplied infinitely in the mirrors—what a spectacle, Don Manuel, the kind that would have challenged the genius of a Tintoretto—we guests all stopped around the proud woman and drank and toasted—another core of servants had carried refreshments—to the happy completion of the palace, in spite of the troublemakers and the jealousy.[26] I was looking at the ceiling, envying the fire—so free and capricious—as it composed and changed its image a thousand times a second with brush strokes more fascinating than any in my sketches, when I felt someone grab me by the arm. It was she, announcing that we should all go look at my improvised studio. I tried to stop her, but my pleas weren't worth a damn. I have never liked to show anyone my unfinished work, to avoid comments or senseless advice and tedious explanations; this time even more. Those meager rough drafts didn't please me at all. But this was no time to make a scene and become the wet blanket on that thrilling trek when she, the leader, in her red and gold sunflowers, was like the fire queen. And that's how we all happened to stop at the music room, provisionally transformed into a painting studio, and now changed into a concert hall, since the servants had set up chairs, drinks, sweets, and even a trio of musicians in one corner who were attacking a piece by Boccherini. Annoyed by the appraisals my work earned from the vain Cornel or the ignorant Costillares, I would have liked to have thrown them and all their squeaky instruments out of there; but since I couldn't do that, I decided to concentrate on listening to the enchanting music of the Maestro. Do you know—well, you may have guessed it last night—that even today I pick up enough of the music so I can enjoy it? But we didn't stay very long, nevertheless, in that halt in the parade. She was on the move again. Inevitably. Everything made her impatient, because of that lively and quick genius that allowed her to understand things and absorb them completely when everyone else had barely begun to catch a glimpse of them. So she sent the musicians away, ordered the servants to continue serving drinks downstairs, and announced that the excursion was over. But . . .

"Just a moment!" she shouted stopping those who were heading up the group. "I forgot to tell you something. Did you know that Fancho can change himself into a dangerous poisoner? Do you know that his seemingly innocent pots of paint hold more poison than the Borgias' lockets and snuff boxes?" I froze. She delivered her harangue so that I wouldn't miss a single syllable, and I didn't understand why she had decided to stage that absurd spectacle. With everyone surprised and bewildered, she leaped like a cat toward the table where my pots were clustered and grabbed up one of the yellows. "See this yellow? If it is Naples yellow, be careful. You could die just by looking at it! And I don't mean your fiancée, Fernando," she added brazenly, turning to the Prince. "God help us! Let's hope that she doesn't bring those bad customs here from Italy![27] And see this innocent purple you usually use to paint the tunic of Jesus of Nazareth? Well it's not so saintly, although it's hypocritically called cobalt violet. Just a whiff of it and the very blood in your veins will be paralyzed!" Exclamations, questions, nervous laughter arose. I was too annoyed to respond, and, of course, deafer than ever. But she kept on. She spun around in her muslins and switched the violet for a green, with the flair of a magician at the fair. She waved the pot under the eyes of the astonished spectators. "And the green! The color of meadows and angels' eyes! Or just the color of Lucifer's eyes? So much the better! Veronese green! Pure poison!" This time she uncorked the flask, remember? And tapping a bit of the powder on to the back of her left fist, she put it up to her nose, that awful gesture that I'd seen her do so many times with the bleached little powder from the Andes. She was about to breathe it in, when I leapt toward her. With one rough blow, slapping her hand, I brushed the little mound of green powder with my left hand and grabbed the pot from her with my right, furious, and shouting: "Are you crazy? This is terrible poison!" "See?" she managed to shout amid the embarrassment of those present since my gesture had been truly violent and since she couldn't keep from crying out when I hit her. And I don't know what we would have done or said then, if another incident hadn't come up to resolve the dangerous situation. Mayte, I'm sorry, your wife, Don Manuel, Her Ladyship, Countess of Chinchón, let out a moan and collapsed; she didn't fall to the ground because her brother, the Cardinal, with lightning reflexes, caught her before she could completely collapse to the floor. There was a commotion. They got her seated in a chair, made room around her so she could breathe, someone called for smelling salts, and Don Fernando handed her a little flask he'd taken from his pocket, but the Cardinal calmed us all down saying: "It's nothing. Just a dizzy spell. She usually gets over them. It could have been the resin from the torches." And as he courteously handed the smelling salts back to the Prince, he brought her back to life patting her lightly on her hands and temples, murmuring a holy incantation, of which I, still rattled, didn't pick up one word. Yes, I remember that at the Cardinal's request, we left them alone in my studio and went back to the hall of mirrors. I have that right, don't I? It was he and not you who helped Her Ladyship, the Countess? Maybe I shouldn't have asked you that . . .

(After so many years, I say to Goya, there is no harm in it. Yes, it was my brother-in-law who helped Mayte. They had been lovingly tied since childhood, and she, I believe, sought refuge in him when the relationship with me was becoming, as it happened, more tense and distant daily. I had helped Mayte, of course—I hadn't quit being a solicitous husband—but he had just gotten in front of me. Goya again excuses himself, saying that he is boring me, since he is describing events to me as if they were new, events I had lived or was present for, the same as he. I tell him that that's not so, what I mean is: not "the same as he," not one of us lives or perceives the same incident the same way. For example, Cayetana's scene in the studio over the poisons seemed an innocent game to me, and Goya's own reaction seemed natural to me and I didn't attribute any more importance to that scene at the time. Another thing is that the following day, when I learned that Cayetana had died from a strange disease that the doctors couldn't agree upon, I hadn't thought about the poisons right away.)

We walked through the parlors and galleries again—the scene was the same as the trip through, but I didn't have the heart for more visual effects—and we went down the staircase. The trio was already playing again in the parlor and everyone sat down to listen; I stood close by since they were playing something very softly, an *adagietto.* I saw the name of the composer on the cellist's score. Haydn, I read. She was still faithful to the late Duke's taste in music.[28] There was a short *rondo.* Applause rewarded the trio. I turned and saw the tall figure, the color of fire, take that opportunity to leave the parlor. I decided to follow her, reproach her, and above all, ask her to forgive me for the scene in the studio. But she was walking, walking very fast. By the time I got to the foot of the stairs, she had already disappeared on the top floor, to the hall of mirrors, and gone into her rooms down the little hallway from the far side; always a swaying flame that seemed to mock her pursuer. I couldn't keep up with her. As I neared my studio, just then your wife and your brother-in-law came out, with a servant lighting the way. And they spent a few minutes talking with me. The Cardinal said to me, "Thank you for your hospitality, Francisco. Let's set a time for you to come visit us in Toledo. Maybe it's time for us to have you do two new portraits.[29] And don't play with poisons." Mayte took him by the arm with a gesture of a frightened little girl, her body so weak again that I was afraid of another swoon, but she whispered, "Good-bye, Francisco, come see us," and they left, escorted by a servant carrying a torch. There were few people in Madrid who called me Francisco, not Fancho, not Paco, not Goya: Francisco. That's what they had learned as children to call me when I painted them for the first time along with their parents, and that's what they continued to call me. I always felt a great affection for them, and they always acted wonderfully toward me. I saw them walk on, arm in arm, taking small steps, through the hall of mirrors, and I remember them that same way—he, always shortening his step to match hers—the way I'd seen them in Arenas de San Pedro, hand in hand, hunting butterflies in the garden, or going to sleep after saying the rosary, under the tender eye of Infante Don Luis. They had walked on by then. I hesitated. She had gone into her chambers, and I didn't dare call to her. Finally, I went back to my studio and decided to do some work.

I must have stayed there around an hour, straightening up the sketches that had been passed from hand to hand, trying to draw a Capricho in which the maja, she, was settling an agreement with an old apothecary, a monstrously deformed version of myself, looking the way I'd just seen myself in the hall of mirrors. Confused, she hesitated, choosing among the pots he offered her. The Capricho was to be called *Which Do You Guarantee?* ambiguously, since although the woman's stance and the old man's lewdness spoke more of potions for love and youth, what the maja was really asking was whether they guaranteed death. In any case, that Capricho didn't get any further than that, a momentary notion, which I tore into a thousand pieces and threw into the wastebasket. I heard the clock at the Order of St. Jerome strike two and decided that it was time to go; a moment before, looking out the window, I'd seen a coach pull away; the guests had started to leave for their homes. I put out the lights and left. In the dark, the hall of mirrors overwhelmed me; I crossed its great length quickly, then the little octagonal hall, and breathed more easily in the gallery where, at least through an open window, some summer night air and din from that ever unsleeping Madrid came in.

Her Ladyship, the Countess, your wife, apparently hadn't recovered from her dizzy spell. She had felt ill, and she had to be carried out. You accompanied her this time. At least that is what Pignatelli whispered to me, his wickedness excited because the Cardinal and Pepita would now have to leave together.

Everyone speculated on what Pepita and the Cardinal would talk about on the way home, while Máiquez played his guitar and Rita sang her familiar little ditties. For the moment, Cayetana had her back turned to me, listening to Rita's song, seated on a footstool, her arm resting on Costillares' thigh. And suddenly, taking advantage of the lull in the applause, she jumped to her feet, like a sudden lively blaze and, grabbing the guitar from Máiquez, started to sing. Now I was looking at her face, how distorted it seemed, the fever in her eyes and the ecstasy of her expression, and the kind of insidious violence that she put into that song that laid bare reasons for love and death. Right away I realized that although I'd kept her from sniffing the Veronese green—which, when all is said and done wasn't a very good joke—she had consoled herself by sniffing the real powder from the Andes. When she was under its influence, she got an energy so artificial and painful—painful to someone who had known her as well as I had and as long as I had—and she lost her natural grace; that incomparable ease turned suddenly colder and shrill, less cordial. Tears began to spout from her eyes while she sang, and I saw with alarm that the black kohl I'd put on her eyelashes was washing over her cheeks. She must have realized it because she quit singing abruptly, handing the guitar back to Máiquez and, stammering the last measures of the song, she left the room where we were sitting. A while later she came back, the damage more or less repaired. She sat down by herself and began to drink glass after glass, while she listened, tense and jealous like a panther, with a surprising lack of compassion, to her cousin Manuelita talking about trousseaux and dates and wedding trips. She adored Manuelita, but her demons had been set in motion. It didn't surprise me when, in another feline impulse, she planted herself in the midst of the gathering, saying, "Oh, child, you're boring us with your engagement stories, and this party is turning into one like Doña Tadea's.[30] We need some excitement around here. A conspiracy! What do you think, Fernando? Or a crime of passion, even if it is only made up, Isidoro, or at least a fire. Where are your troublemakers, Costillares? Will they forgive me for the palace if I hire them to liven up my parties?" All of a sudden, I saw a spark in her eyes. And I was alarmed. It could have meant anything. "But what do I need them for?" she cried out. She ran toward one of the torches that lit up the room, grabbed it from its stand and turning to face us, Pignatelli, Costillares, me, we who knew her too well and were getting ready to intervene, she cried, "I can set my own house on fire!" She lunged toward the curtains and we toward her, and she struggled amid cries and laughter. We laughed, too, to lighten up the situation, and finally Costillares managed to grab her from behind, by the elbows, and Pignatelli retrieved the torch, while I poured water from a flower vase on the first little flames that were dancing on the brocade. The Osuna woman had gotten to her feet and had gone over to the Cardinal, begging him tacitly to intervene; Máiquez played a few mock tragic chords on the guitar, singing about the melodrama being played out there; Cornel was nodding off, drunk, I imagine, on some cushions; Prince Fernando hadn't lost his amused and stupid expression; Manuelita was clinging to her fiancé; there I was like a fool, vase in one hand and roses in the other.[31]

She seemed to give in to being conquered, not so much because of what we'd done but because something inside her had gone limp, abandoned, suddenly, as always. Nothing was worth the effort. Not her palace, not the party, not us. She shook herself loose from Costillares, laughed a bit, for appearance' sake, slowly gathered up her cashmere shawl. She left without saying a word, in an atmosphere of failure and sadness that surprised me. The guests exchanged some knowing and ironic glances; someone woke up Cornel, telling him it was time to leave, and Pignatelli, being a member of the household, took charge of seeing everyone out. When we got to the vestibule, I looked up. The high ceilings and the top of the staircase were dark, gloomy. There was a blur on the top of the stairway. It looked like the cashmere shawl to me, like a spot of blood on the Carrara marble.

(In the last parts of his story, Goya has grown sorrowful and disheartened. Strange, this hasn't aged him. The memory of his passion—if it is memory—is so intense that I have the impression of seeing before me a person at the same time vigorous and vulnerable: a wounded bull.)

Notes

16. As we recall, those three people, plus Don Carlos Pignatelli, the Duchess's two personal physicians, and Doña Catalina Barajas, her chambermaid, were the heirs to whom the Duchess left her personal wealth in a will drawn up five years before—the sixteenth of February 1797—in Sanlúcar de Barrameda. This shows that this was not the first time the Duchess had thought about her death.
17. According to the chronicles, there were several fires set at the Buenavista Palace while it was under construction.
18. Isidoro Máiquez and Rita Luna were famous actors who worked as a team; Costillares was one of the best bullfighters of his day; the Count and Countess of Benavente-Osuna represented the most illustrious, and at the same time worldly, of the old Spanish nobility. The Countess especially was a woman of great splendor, truly rivaling the Duchess of Alba in the last splendors of that Bourbon Court.
19. The embarrassing episode questions Godoy's ability to reconcile his many parallel lives, which he later boasts about. (Later in this Memoir we shall see a letter from the statesman, Jovellanos, who, while agreeing with Godoy's efforts to keep the Bonapartes from the Spanish throne, also questions Godoy's discretion in personal matters.) In bygone days, it would have been called crass indifference.

20. Goya met her when she was very young. In the dawn of his career as a world-famous painter, he painted Infante Don Luis (Carlos III's brother) with his morganatic family, his wife and their children, around 1783, in their country mansion at Arenas de San Pedro. There is a family portrait, in which everyone appears, as well as an individual portrait of María Teresa (done in the same year), which bears this inscription: "Her Ladyship S. D. María Teresa, daughter of Sr. Infante Don Luis at the age of two years and nine months." This explains why Goya, nineteen years later, still calls her Mayte.

21. Despite the ease with which she handled the invitation, Cayetana de Alba had probably taken it for granted that Godoy would attend with his legitimate wife and that it had been Pepita's presence that upset everything.

22. Manuelita de Silva y Waldstein, who married the Count of Haro before she was fourteen years old, was painted by Goya a year later (as we will see) and died in 1805. She was closely related, by paternal ties, to the Duchess, whose family names were Silva and Álvarez de Toledo.

23. For the first time Godoy acknowledges explicitly something that until now, for scholars, has been mere reason for speculation, based on rumors written down by chroniclers of the day, in the famous jealous letter from the Queen, etc.

24. Either the Countess-Duchess later gave up on her project or Goya who, fifteen years before, had painted for her his popular scenes for the alameda and, five years before, his no-less-famous six scenes of witchcraft, excused himself from doing a third series. Let's not forget that after the Duchess's death, Goya quit painting for a long time, according to his own declaration.

25. A new allusion to the murderer's motive. Now, at least, we know that Godoy identified the murderer as one of his companions at the Duchess's dinner party.

26. For those who are shocked by the armies of servants that, according to Goya's account, the Duchess turned out to have, let's just say that, at her death, there were more than three hundred servants in her service.
27. An imprudent—or extremely opportunistic, depending on how one looks at it—allusion by the Duchess to the bad reputation that the Court of Naples enjoyed concerning a very liberal use of poison. Let's not forget that, as is documented in the correspondence between Godoy and Napoleon and even in the correspondence of María Luisa herself, and in Godoy's first Memoirs, the three years between Fernando's marriage and the death of his wife, Princess María Antonia of Naples, were years of constant concern for the Queen, who feared being poisoned at any time by her daughter-in-law, on orders from the King and Queen of Naples. Ironically, the circumstances of the death of the Princess, who died of tuberculosis, fearing to eat anything that did not pass her strict scrutiny ("her mania for eating lettuce, straight vinegar, mozzarella pie with a lot of pepper," as the Queen herself says in a letter), aroused suspicions about her mother-in-law to which Godoy himself opens a path. This whole story is suggested by "Naples yellow."
28. The Duke of Alba died in 1795 when still young; a little while after Goya painted a beautiful portrait of him in which he appears leafing through a score by Haydn.
29. Goya painted Luis and María Teresa de Borbón y Vallábriga many times: in 1783, as we have said, when they were six and three years old, respectively, in a family portrait; and each in separate portraits, which comprise a pair; there is also a pair of portraits of Luis, already Cardinal, and María Teresa, already engaged to Godoy, painted in 1797, similar to those Goya would paint of a husband and wife of the nobility or of a bourgeois couple, and similar to those he painted of them in 1800. Goya never got to paint these "new portraits" the

Cardinal mentions. The ones from 1800 are the last done of the pair.

30. Could this be Doña Tadea Arias de Henríquez, whom Goya painted eight years before?

31. The chronicles of the day record the Duchess's frenzy, torch in hand, threatening her guests with burning the palace herself. They only differ a bit in the words they attribute to her: "With my own hands, I'm going to do what everyone else wants to do."

GOYA'S STORY

III

At some point, at the beginning of the evening, we had agreed with her on a meeting for the next day, at midday. I was to start the work up again. We would revise the sketches, discuss new ideas, and if necessary I would begin again from the beginning, but "get it into your head, Fancho," she had said to me, "I want to unveil the palace as soon as possible; Napoleon may invade us at any moment." The joke had been applauded by her staff, although the curate did cross himself. No one suspected then that some years later her joke would become a tragic reality. But she didn't get to see it, and we didn't remember that joke either, not the secretary, the treasurer, or I. She wouldn't even get to live to the next night; she would die even before the roses died.

I arrived at the palace around two, after loafing around the paseo. Looking at the palace and its gardens through the grills on the window, I thought it was strange how quiet everything was. Although construction was halted until September, she had so many servants you could always see scores of them coming and going. Entering by the door on Empress Street, I was even more surprised to recognize Don Jaime Bonells, her aging personal physician, who had attended the Duke in 1795, going out the door on Empress Street and leaving in his barouche. But since she called him if one of her staff or servants had the slightest complaint, I still had no reason for concern. There were not many moments of peace left, though. In the vestibule I ran into Pignatelli and Catalina,[32] who had just seen Bonells off. They were talking in low voices, with a discreet air; Catalina ran up the stairs, without saying hello to me. When Pignatelli saw me, all he did was wrinkle his brow into a frown and point expressively and dolefully with his right finger to the upper floor and hang his head somberly. After that he went out to the street, leaving me alone with my uneasiness. There wasn't a servant in sight. I was surprised, now that they were empty, at how vast the vestibule looked and how high the stairway seemed. No noise drifted down to me from the long hallways or from the upper floor. The palace was so large that you could be dancing or suffering in it and no one would know. I sat down on a chair left there for some petitioner. I looked at the walls, the ceiling; right then I knew perfectly well that I was never going to paint them. A good twenty minutes went by; then on the cobblestones I felt the sound of another coach approaching. A minute later, Pignatelli let in the other house doctor, Don Francisco Durán, the one whom she had preferred to have attend her the past few years. Not taking any notice of me, the two turned toward the stairs and started up. Catalina appeared at the top and came down the stairs to meet Durán. The three disappeared quickly. I went up the stairs two at a time and got to the top in time to see them leave the corridor. Her suite began at the far end of the hall of mirrors, across from the little octagonal parlor. My workshop was located just in front of the door they had left open, practically in the path of whomever came or went to rooms in the rest of the palace. Before I started to track down Catalina and the two men—they had been so wrapped up in each other they hadn't noticed my following them—I decided to go to my workshop and wait there. I was sure Catalina would come to show the doctor out in a minute, and I could approach her.

I ran over to a table and a stool, pretending to work; from there I could keep track of anyone coming through the hall of mirrors. A long time went by; I tried in vain to stay calm and above all not to draw any conclusions. But inevitably I was thinking that an overdose of that fiendish powder from the Andes could explain this coming and going of doctors and these distressed looks. I don't know when I casually looked down at the table where my paint pots were lined up like an army of foot soldiers. I had a sudden flash, and I dashed over to those pots. The Veronese green was missing. That couldn't be. But it was gone. I looked again. It was missing. Maybe yesterday, when I was straightening up, I put it in the wrong place. It was missing. I closed my eyes and took a deep breath. I tried to calm down. I looked at all the pots one by one. I stared hard at the Naples yellow and the silver white and the cobalt violet, telling myself: Now the blessed green will turn up, this is just a mistake, clouded vision. But it was missing. I backed away, unsteady on my legs. I felt for the stool. My hands were icy; my throat was dry and tight. I was shaking, sweating. What had she said that evening? "You have your violets and your greens to finish me off . . . "

(Goya has started to tremble. His temples are perspiring. His voice has become weak and raspy. He closes his eyes, as if to ward off a dizzy spell. It's terrible. I am trembling, too. I too know that someone has stolen the poison. We are not in Bordeaux. We are in Madrid, in another workshop, and the Veronese green is missing from the pots of paint.)

When I got over my confusion, I could see that many people had gathered in the hall of mirrors: the chaplain, the treasurer, the secretary, various maids and butlers, and Manuelita Silva, pale and frightened. Some were gathered around Catalina, others around Pignatelli. I didn't have to ask anyone anything. She was in the throes of death. In the mirrors, you could see, half-open, the door that went to her suite. I went slowly toward it. No one paid any attention to me. No one realized some seconds later that I had slipped into her private chambers, which consisted basically of two large rooms: the bedroom and a small salon, or antechamber, that served as both a dressing room and boudoir. I had just slipped into this latter room; no one was in it. The door to her bedroom was half-closed. The room was all in shadows; the blinds filtered the light from the west on that summer afternoon, light in grooves that broke against the curtains and the marble statues. And suddenly I saw the glass. There, on the dressing table, the glass, with one of those grooves of light refracted in it, blinding me as it struck the crystal. A priceless Venetian goblet, a gift from a papal ambassador, a goblet with blues and gold intertwined in an intricate arabesque around two medallions of very fine smalt. I had always admired it; now it hypnotized me. Without thinking, I went right over to it. I didn't touch it. The goblet was half-full of a green liquid, of course. I say of course because I would have seen green no matter what, I was so convinced that there was a tie not only logical but also mysterious, magical, between the missing paint and the goblet that beckoned me. I say that too because the light refracted in the crystal and in the liquid was mixing the blues and golds, making a small cavity inside the glass—glaucous, ultramarine. Green!

My instinct, more than my hearing, made me turn around. The door to the bedroom was open, and as if someone called to them, Catalina and Manuelita came in from the parlor. The doctor conferred a second with them—they still didn't know I was there, as if I were a ghost—and then he went back into the bedroom with Catalina. Little Manuelita, to control her distress, sat down in a chair against the wall, next to the door, and waited. It was then that she saw me and smiled, looking totally abandoned. I think she said, "Death is taking her from us . . . " But I'm not sure. Perhaps it was just what I was dreading to hear. Shaken, I had to lean against the dressing table for support. I looked at the goblet and back at Manuelita. We both looked away at the same instant. And we stayed that way, she, seated like a little child doing penitence for the Mother Superior, I, standing immobile out of confusion and pain; that's how we were sitting when Catalina and the doctor returned. "She wants to see you two," Catalina said, and seeing my stupor, explained: "You, too, Don Fancho." Manuelita had already disappeared into the bedroom. The doctor was washing his hands in the wash basin, and Catalina handed him a towel. With a sudden pitying look, that man who seemed so cold took her by the arms, not saying a word. There was no hope. An irrational impulse came over me: grab the goblet, take it with me, hide it, as if from back in her bedroom she were begging me to do it. I'd wait until Durán left. Catalina would go with him. Then I would do it. I began to think about how I would take it from there so no one would notice; maybe no one would have cared at all; so overcome by all their anguish they probably didn't even know that that goblet was there. But Catalina and Durán went on and on with their hand-washing ritual, and Manuelita was already coming out. Was I mistaken? Did the dear, anguished eyes really linger a fraction of a second on the dressing table as she came out of the bedroom? I didn't have time to think twice about it. Catalina was urging me to go into the bedroom. There the goblet remained. I was on my way to see its victim.

(I keep quiet about the goblet. I don't tell Goya anything. I don't tell him that I had held it in my hands the night before, when it was still an innocent Venetian goblet from the quattrocento, as I admired the lady and the stag in its two very lovely smalt medallions. I don't tell him that today I still see it, sparkling, magic, just as he says, and tragic at the same time, there on Cayetana's dressing table.)

Will you forgive me if I don't tell you what we talked about in my last conversation with her? I can only tell you that despite her suffering, despite the anguish of her body and soul, despite that ashen face and those eyes burning with fever, she was the same as always, witty even in delirium . . . witty even with God and death . . . "I wanted it this way, dearest Fancho," she said to me, "only maybe just not so fast . . . " But I don't want to talk about that.

(Goya, clearly, has difficulties going on with his story. I am about to tell him not to continue, when again he manages to find his voice, a tone that is weak and that breaks, dry and ragged, like baked clay.)

After that I left her room. I fell into a chair, my head on my chest, far away from what was going on around me. There was a rustling of skirts and whispered conversations. Other people came in: Pignatelli, the chaplain, Bonells, the old doctor who had left no more than two hours ago. The curate had brought with him a covered chalice, to give the Last Rites, He set it on the dressing table, making room among jewels and perfume. Then I realized that the goblet was not in its place. It had disappeared. No one had touched anything in that room, where all anyone talked about was death, but nevertheless someone had gone to the trouble of taking it from its place . . . But, who? Catalina? Could she have . . . ? As a reply, she leaned out the bedroom door and beckoned for the curate. Surely she had gone in as I left. Everyone realized that Cayetana was dying. The room was filled with people. The Osuna woman, Haro, the inconsolable Manuelita, and Costillares had shown up. Pignatelli was crying. Bargas fell defeated into a chair. Berganza was gnawing his fist. I backed into a corner and there, in the shadow, I couldn't shake my surprise, astounded by her death. I felt a light breeze that had filtered through the sheer curtains blow across my forehead; it seemed to be sweeping all away, softly and slowly, forever. I don't know how long I stood there. I know what wrenched me from that state. A light, blinding me once again. The goblet was back in the same place as before, brilliant, on the dressing table. By magic it had vanished, and by magic it had materialized again, teasing me with its diamond lights. I walked around the dresser, more fascinated than with some complex theory. Just when I was about to touch it, I saw to my amazement that it no longer contained any liquid at all. It had been emptied and dried. I couldn't bring myself to pick it up. The fingers I pulled away were burning. I looked around me to see if anyone had seen my gesture. In a corner, the Count of Haro was consoling Manuelita. Her eyes looked lost, as if she were looking through me, seeing a ghost; she was flooded with pain. SHE had died.

(I think Goya is crying. He is breathing hard, with a deaf fury, but I stay put. The silence grows very long. He fills a glass with brandy and forgets again to offer me any. I make a move to show that I mean to end the conversation and leave, but he stops me with a brisk wave of his weathered hand. He wants to finish his story. And I want to hear it to the very end.)

A bad dream that began when I arrived at the palace was ending with a terrible awakening. SHE had died. And I knew how. But if I had had the good sense and the clear sight to cry out when I discovered my pot of paint was missing—then, when she was still alive—it made no sense to say it now, when there was no fixing what had happened, now that Catalina and the other maids had begun to lay her out and now that the doctors couldn't reach an agreement and were talking about the miasmas of summer, about a virulent infection, about contagion from yellow fever, brought secretly from the south. Never once mentioning the word poison. The word that had certainly obsessed her that evening, from the moment when I surprised her smearing her neck with silver white until I knocked the green powder from her hand. These were my last two physical contacts with her, because on her death bed she hadn't let me come near her, but I have already said I don't want to talk about that.

At the funeral the rumors going around reached me: She had died from poison, and the murdering hand, the one that had poured that venom drop by drop in her glass the night of her last party, was the same anonymous hand who lit the fires, a punishment from the people, then; or was that hand yours, Don Manuel, spurred on all the way from La Granja by the Queen, a punishment from higher up, then?[33] Do you think that I ought to have gone myself to the police and told what I knew: That a poison had disappeared, a goblet had been washed carefully, and that she had toyed with the idea of dying from Naples yellow or from silver white in my studio and later in the palace? What would my statement have proved? What would have been gained? An investigation, maybe . . . (It was conducted anyway, but I didn't know that until later.) And what could have come from that? To prove that there was a lethal poison lost in the palace? A scandal, supporting some suspicions that I knew to be calumnious . . . But why go on looking for reasons? I kept quiet for only one reason, one so irresistible, so powerful, that it has made me silent, quiet for twenty years. I kept quiet because her death was a secret between her and me. The last. Maybe . . . the only one.

I went back to the palace, to my studio. Her heirs (the will had already been opened) had hired me for a mural for her mausoleum. That's when I learned that there had been an investigation. But to its negative results was added the fact that none of the members of the household gave any credence to the rumors.[34] I holed up and devoted myself to my work. Conquering my aversion, I armed myself with perseverance and sketched the mural. In the midst of all this tragedy there was only one consolation: Her will included a legacy for my son, Javier, an obligation her heirs were to carry out for all his life.[35] My satisfaction didn't stem so much from the legacy itself as from the fact that she had drawn up the will in Sanlúcar, in February 1797, which was the height and the happiest moment of our relationship. Despite my jealousy, the rupture, the separation, my thoughtless actions, my . . . "caprichos," to put it another way, she had never been moved to cancel the legacy. In this way, she had been faithful, completely, far beyond what I, in my blindness, had suffered as infidelities and deficiencies.

I was working on the sketch one afternoon, when Pignatelli appeared in the studio. He had radically changed his attitude toward me since her death. Now he treated me with a deep and sad affection that, I believe, was an attempt, like so many others we engaged in, to keep her alive in the palace. He had come to tell me that Javier's legacy had gone into effect that very morning and that they, the heirs, were ready to carry it out with the same lasting goodwill that she would have shown. Accordingly, they had agreed to give me a crystal goblet that she always used in her excursions. With the approval of Catalina and Bargas, the treasurer, it should, as she had suggested many times, pass into my hands if she should die before I. It was a posthumous request. They had decided, then, to fulfill it. I knew what goblet they were talking about. We two had drunk from it, for the first time, on the road to Sanlúcar, in the spring of 1796, and that had been the sweet start of other intimacies. And I smiled as I remembered that she had expressed her wish to her household, as if everyone knew the reason why I fancied the goblet. Six years had passed, a breakup, a death, and now that token from the past of fleeting but complete happiness was coming back to me. I accepted the generous offer. After some comment on my work, Pignatelli said to me as he was leaving, "Talk with Catalina, Don Fancho, she has the goblet." At the moment I wasn't thinking about anything but that stop along the road, near Écija, about the picnic under the trees, far from the chapel and from Catalina, about Cayetana, drinking from the goblet with her full, rosy mouth and raising her eyes toward me, holding the goblet out to me and saying, "Goya, drink . . ." She didn't call me Fancho yet.[36]

That night I looked for Catalina in her quarters on the first floor and she, busy as she was—she always was—left her work and offered to give me the goblet. She led me through the hallways toward the chapel. Before we came to it, she stopped in front of a small door, took out her handful of keys, picked out one and opened the door. Although the door was small, the room it led to wasn't. It was a kind of fantastic bazaar where the riches that were meant to decorate the palace, all the treasures that she had gone about snatching from her other homes, buying at auctions, acquiring from antique dealers, or ordering from Paris, Milan, Venice, and even faraway Istanbul, were gathered. I'm not going to describe those riches, although they deserve it. But picture, Don Manuel, all the splendor imaginable—tapestries, porcelain, smalt, arms, clocks, marble statues, paintings crystal, lamps, divans, incense burners . . .[37] Catalina opened a closet; in it were arranged ceramic, porcelain, and glass goblets, single pieces that didn't make up a set. You could find all styles, shapes, and colors there. "It was this one, right?" Catalina said, putting her hands on the one that was truly the goblet she used on her country picnics, a Bavarian goblet, I think, made of thick, white and ruby adamantine crystal, but another goblet on a higher shelf drew my gaze as if by a magnet: a blue and gold goblet, Venetian, with rich smalt . . . Never in my life had I lied with such aplomb. "No, it was that one, the blue one," I assured her, "I was there when the nuncio gave it to her. I made over it so much that she would have given it to me right there, she told me, if it wouldn't have been an insult to the prelate." Part of that statement was true—I had been there when she accepted the gift, I had admired the delicate, masterful work—but I do not think that that partial truth gave enough strength to my lie. Catalina, who was a strictly honest person and who I'm sure believed I was too, looked at me, baffled but for just an instant. Right away she became resolute, picked up the Venetian goblet and put it in my hands. "Then here it is," she said. "Her wish was for you to have it." The transaction was settled.

(Goya is suddenly an old man. Worn out, bent over, trembling. Remembering the theft of the goblet had drained him of his energy, as if in that moment, exchanging the goblet of love for the goblet of death, he himself had begun to die. He started talking again, and you would say I had guessed his thoughts. I had never seen him look older.)

Exchanging the goblet, I had renounced a very sweet secret, shared with her, for another shared, but unfortunate secret; owning the goblet, which I hid in my studio out of sight of the whole world, was something of a cancer during those months of total depression, when I couldn't take up a brush again except to do the despairing if unswerving work of finishing the mural for her pantheon.[38] The silence around me had grown more dense than ever, since it was born and fed from my inconsolable privation, from my horror. Until something came to draw me out of my paralysis. An army doctor named Don José Queraltó showed up at my studio one day that hard winter, wanting to have his portrait done. I knew him a little and at first I said no, but just as he was leaving, I suddenly remembered that he had won a great name as an expert in pharmacological and chemical research. I realized that he was the man I needed. I accepted the job. When we agreed on the price of the portrait, he didn't know that to my fee he would add a little work in his field of expertise. I took the goblet out of its hiding place and began to examine its bottom, the sediment that time had dried up and which was nearly invisible. I hadn't wanted to ask my own doctors to do it; the lie that I needed to carry out would have seemed too flagrant. And of course I hadn't wanted to involve Bonells or Durán either. Now, unexpectedly, the problem was resolving itself. One afternoon, I showed up at Queraltó's home with the goblet wrapped in a piece of linen. I told him a story of a mischievous young child and an imprudent game with my paints; I had washed the goblet afterward, but I was afraid that there was residue in the bottom, that someone could drink from it and be poisoned. With a scalpel, Queraltó scraped up a bit of material and put it right on the lens of the magnifying glass so he could observe it. At our next sitting he told me what he'd found. It was arsenate of copper in a nearly pure form. He advised me, "Don't drink out of it, Maestro. Anyway, this goblet is too lovely to use around the house, right?"

That same month of January, I had another visitor.

Manuelita Silva, the brand-new Countess of Haro, appeared in my studio accompanied by her husband, the Count, wanting me to do a portrait of her, too. Her cousin's heirs had made that decision, too, carrying out a wish she'd declared many times: that that portrait be a wedding present. This had been spelled out at some prior date, certainly with the greatest discretion, because of the mourning, which the Silvas owed to their illustrious relative; but now, six months later, they were coming for their posthumous present. Given the circumstance, it was very hard for me to say no. It was her wish, and I couldn't stand in the way. But, besides, I confess—and I don't know if I was influenced by Queraltó's recent findings—it weighed heavily on me that it was Manuelita who asked me to do it, Manuelita, whose frightened and tearful eyes I had never managed to untangle completely from the fleeting disappearance of the goblet and from its unexplained washing. So, this time too, a second time that year, I gave in and accepted the project. With only one condition: The portrait had to be painted in my studio, because the doctors had forbidden me to go out in the winter cold. That excuse about the doctors was a new lie. Manuelita agreed to pose in the studio several afternoons. From the very first, the blue and gold goblet was on my work table, in plain sight, so that from where I stood to paint I could always see how it affected the girl.

I saw her reaction at the first sitting. Her little childlike mouth was opened in a convulsive grin, a stupor, her cheeks turned scarlet, her eyes narrowed as if to make sure she wasn't seeing things. It took great effort for her to hold the pose, her eyes fixed on me under the Hellenized hairdo we had agreed on. Not long after, she made some excuse, a problem with her crepe stole, I believe, to get up from her chair and casually walk over to my table to confirm her first impression. Then in the following session she didn't try to hide her feelings. Before she went into the dressing room to change, she asked me suddenly, "That goblet, isn't it like one that my cousin Cayetana had?" I had my answer ready. "It's the same one. She left it to me when she died. It was on her dressing table the last day. She had drunk from it, but it could never be proved what she had drunk, because a concerned hand took it and washed it before she died." It was a new lie. The police never found out that the goblet existed. But my words were enough; the tender creature posed that whole session in a state of constant nervousness, her inquisitive eyes going back and forth from the goblet to me. And as hard as I tried, I couldn't keep that portrait from showing, in the sweetness of her childlike face, that tension in her long neck, that fearful questioning in her dark eyes.[39]

At her last sitting, after she had changed into her winter street clothes and a little hood that made her look even more like a child, just as she was about to leave, she couldn't contain herself anymore and sat down on a stool, wringing her hands inside the little fur muff. "I have to tell someone, and I'd rather it be you, Don Fancho. You loved her as much as I did. You have the goblet, and it seems to me that you have already figured something out." I had knelt down in front of her, begging with only my posture that, now that she had decided to talk, she do it so I wouldn't miss a single syllable. She raised the muff to her chin and began. She seemed like a little girl confessing some mischief, like stealing some chocolates or breaking some figurine.

"Remember that Cayetana wanted to see you and me before she died, Don Fancho? Well, I went into her room. She sat up, disheveled among the covers, pulled out a little snuff box and put it in my hands. She said to me, 'Make this disappear, throw it away, anywhere you want, burn it, but don't let anyone see it. Not anyone.' I took the little box, trembling. I was shocked by her deathly appearance and by the intense way she spoke to me. I realized it was the last time I would see Cayetana. How could someone fall apart so fast in just one night? 'It's a medicine that I'm taking behind the doctors' backs,' she told me, 'and those fools would end up saying that I have poisoned myself.' So, that was it, I thought. Poison. That explained it all. From that moment I had no doubts that cousin Cayetana had . . ." Her fear, her grief was so great, she couldn't say the word. Anguished, she took a breath with difficulty. "I was still very scared from the night before: all that melodrama in your studio about the poisons. Then the episode with the torch, when she really seemed bent on setting the palace on fire; but more than that, at the end, when she left without saying good-bye to anyone, going up that stairway like someone going up a gallows . . . I hadn't been able to get to sleep, I was so upset by her low spirits, by her solitude. Meanwhile, she had swallowed that poison that I now had in my hands, inside that little, innocent-looking box . . . Ideas crowded together in my head. I think at that point, I remembered the goblet on her dressing table that you, Don Fancho, were looking at with such misgivings . . . And I saw her, in a shining halo, slowly drinking down the poison in the goblet even while we were getting into our coaches . . . 'What are you thinking about?' she asked me. 'Will you do what I ask?' And when I had calmed her down and told her I would do it, she said good-bye to me. 'Now go,' she said. 'I don't know if I'll get well by your wedding, but for God's sake, don't postpone it on my account. Your fiancé is charming. He's handsome, distinguished, and intelligent. If I were ten years younger, you wouldn't be the only one in love with him. Go, go on, and be happy, dear girl.' I took the handkerchief that Manuelita had pulled out of the muff and dried her tears myself over the smile her cousin's loving joke again provoked. She concluded very gravely, "When I left her room, the first thing I saw was the goblet, and in your eyes, Don Fancho, certainly, that you knew the truth, no matter how well I kept the little box hidden tight in my fist. You wanted to make the poison disappear, too. But you had to go into the bedroom. In the meantime, Catalina and the doctor left, and I was left alone there, with the goblet. I didn't have any time to lose. I threw the cashmere shawl that she had used that morning over my shoulders and hid the goblet, along with the little box, under my arm. In a corner away from the hall of mirrors, I could hide the little box and empty the goblet in the dirt of a planter. No one had seen me. Just then, my fiancé appeared . . . my husband . . . and we went to Cayetana's room together. Everyone was crowded in there, upset, talking in low voices. She was dying. I don't even know how or when I put the goblet back in its place. I only knew that I had carried out her last wish. And when I discovered you looking at me, Don Fancho, I tried to tell you with my eyes: It's done now, it's done, the way she wanted it. It's a secret between us—her, you, and me. I'm right, aren't I? You also believe that cousin Cayetana poisoned herself?"

I lied. I said that I didn't believe it. That all the story about the goblet was just her imagination, and I had only noticed that she'd washed the goblet, since I had seen it sitting on the dressing table. And that the little snuff box—and here I didn't have to lie—held some powders that I knew about, powder that hadn't caused her death. She didn't say anything more, as if not to break the fragile and unlikely miracle of my words. She dried her last tears, arranged her curls, put her hands in the muff, and stood up. "Good-bye, Don Fancho," she mumbled. And she left. She chose to accept my version of the facts without argument rather than to go on thinking that her beloved Cayetana had killed herself. Although I knew that she was not very convinced when she left, I think in any case I envied her for her deception. I didn't see her again. Two years later I learned that she had died giving birth. Poor, sweet child. Dr. Queraltó died around then, too, did you know? That goblet seemed to keep its harmful powers. Except for me, it finished off all those who touched it. But don't pay any attention to me. I'm superstitious, like any good campesino.[40]

With the last brush strokes to Manuelita's portrait, my story comes to an end, Don Manuel. Now you know it all. Except, perhaps, the underlying reasons for the way I've acted, the reasons for keeping so quiet for more than twenty years and for talking now. Why didn't I talk? Because of that mysterious pact that we set up over the goblet, while she was suffering in the next room . . . Because of that secret she confided in me without telling it to me . . . Illusion of someone in love, if you like. As if in her farewell she had made a gesture—of recognition, complicity, gratitude—so I was consoled by being her trustee, having shared that last moment of her heart. But she wanted, demanded the secret. As she proved, including the strange desire to make the innocent powders from the Andes disappear. Perhaps in her delirium she had confused one poison with another. And why did I want to tell you this now? Time has passed. The world has healed. I don't need to grapple with that fantasy anymore. And I ought to consider the poor King and Queen, who are still charged with too much blame that wasn't theirs. That includes you, too. You, who are going to write those memoirs, who must do so, who will have the power to cleanse the Queen's name of all the trash that they have sullied her with . . .

(Goya goes on talking. I half listen to him. Perhaps I do not believe enough in what he is telling me. I ask myself what the true and deep need is that brings Goya to break the pact . . .)

We have to order our concerns before we die, Don Manuel. To free ourselves of some things, too. Set fire to others. Like she did, with her torch.

(Goya stares straight into the flame of a candle that is burning down.)

Notes

32. Catalina Barajas, the Duchess's chambermaid, and, as we have seen, one of the seven heirs.

33. We should establish once and for all that death by poisoning was common coin in Europe in those days. Without going into the black legend of the Borgias, which includes a poisoning pope, the Paracelso case, or the very famous *affaire des poisons* that upset France in 1679 and in which Mme. de Montespan, Louis XIV's lover, was implicated, there were at least four cases in the Spanish Court itself at the end of the eighteenth and beginning of the nineteenth century in which serious rumors about poisoning were circulated: An attempt against Jovellanos (1797); the death of the Duchess of Alba (1802); Queen María Luisa's prolonged and vivid fears, as we have seen, of being poisoned by her daughter-in-law, María Antonia of Naples, and at the instigation of her in-laws (1802–1805); the death of the Princess María Antonia herself, which rumors attributed to her mother-in-law, who, if she had poisoned the Princess, would have found final relief from her own fears (1805). In the not-too-distant past (1791), in Vienna, none other than Mozart feared in his agony that he had been poisoned; posterity has not discarded the idea that his assassin was Maestro Salieri, the Emperor's Master of Chapel. In those days,

death by poisoning was known in the Austrian court as "the Italian disease."

34. According to some chroniclers, some suspected that the Duchess's death had been caused by her seven heirs, who, so the rumors went, had gotten together in an unlikely meeting and decided to "eliminate" their benefactress. Either Goya was not aware of that eccentric idea, or he had forgotten it in 1825. He seems obsessed only by the fact that suspicion had fallen on the Queen and on Godoy; it is this that best explains his late confession.

35. In the sealed will the Duchess drew up, Javier, the painter's son, does appear as beneficiary. He is declared legatee as the sixteenth and last obligation imposed on her heirs: to give "to the son of Don Francisco de Goya, ten reales daily for life."

36. A letter from Marianito, Goya's grandson, son of Javier and Gumersinda Goicoechea, to Carderara, to whom he appealed from time to time to sell some antiques with which he was paid, reads: "My dear sir: Finding myself short of funds and knowing you to be an enthusiast of old things, I remit to you a goblet that the once Duchess of Alba, Da. Ma. Teresa de Silva, always used on trips and country outings. On her death, she left it to my grandfather for him to keep as a memento." Comments from family members show that Goya did own the Venetian goblet and the reasons for their letting him have it, but which in truth applied to a different goblet.

37. Don Manuel can certainly imagine it, since he acquired some of the richest pieces from the Duchess's treasury. How could Goya have forgotten that?

38. The mural has disappeared from its original place: the Duchess's pantheon in the Padres Misioneros del Salvador Church, known as the Church of the Novitiate. There remains only a sketch, probably the one that Goya was doing when Pignatelli appeared to offer him the goblet.

39. The study of the Countess of Haro's portrait confirms Goya's words exactly: Despite the young model's undeniable charm, tension and apprehension appear in her neck and eyes.
40. Both the Countess and Dr. Queraltó were painted, as is supposed, at the beginning of 1803, in the middle of winter, and did die in 1805. With them disappeared two of the three witnesses who could have spoken on the matter of the poisoned goblet. Outside of a supposed murderer . . .

MY STORY

MY STORY
I

I LEFT Bordeaux the next morning.

I called the coachman and the postboy when it was not even four. The coachman was sleeping off a hangover, no doubt. He got up annoyed, babbling and slow-witted. He could not understand that we were leaving and that he had to harness the team and load the luggage. The post-boy was not at the inn; he arrived just in time to get on his horse and leave. Throughout the entire first leg of the trip, the two took advantage of any opportunity to close their eyes and get some sleep, even if it were a second, while I, who had also slept very little, was wide awake, agitated, unceasingly assaulted by the images that that old man had known how to awaken by evoking that night so long ago in Buenavista, a palace I later lived in for a few years. However, never were the memories as vivid and goading as now, so long afterward, instigated by Don Fancho's martyred memory.[1]

It would have served no purpose to go back to see him again, if I did not sit him before me and say: Don Fancho, you are wrong. You have lived all these years deceived. Don't torment yourself anymore. Cayetana did not commit suicide; they killed her. But I could not tell him that, without telling him the truth, without answering his tale with my own, so similar and so different, the same story in a different light, the same but different, the right side and the wrong side of the events, the true crime caught in the shadow, the unbearable burden of the tree of knowledge, fruit that perhaps I alone had bitten into . . . and, of course, the murderer. But I could not tell him that. I did nothing more than leave him a brief farewell note. The postboy slipped it under the door at Maison Poc.

So I found myself traveling through France again, en route to Nice, closed up in my coach, blind now to the beauties of the landscape, to Provence's agreeable climate, to the magnificent countryside that had sheltered Pius VII, to all the road was offering me as distraction from my obsessive reminiscences of that party in the Buenavista Palace. But my memories were soaring, unrestrained, farther back to the start of the tragedy. Back to 1797.

They had been peaceful times for Spain, despite some black storm clouds on the horizon. In 1795, peace with France and with Prussia at Basel had been won; the treaty of San Ildefonso with France had been signed. Already Prince of Peace by then, I managed to give a learned slant to my government; I had even gotten the appointment as minister from the distinguished lawyer and encyclopedist Jovellanos, a man the uprising had found so hard to stomach. Negotiations of state impassioned me, and I dedicated my energies to those negotiations without moderation. Nevertheless, by then, my personal life had become satisfying, exciting, and more tangled up than a fistful of cherries. A year before I had met Pepita Tudó, and my love for that girl, all verve and life, had gained ground on prudence. No one in the palace, not even the King and Queen themselves—am I right when I say the Queen was the first to figure us out?—was unaware of the ties of intimacy that very quickly united me to the devilish girl from Cádiz. And no doubt it was that indiscretion that hastened the Monarchs to carry out an old and vague project: marrying me off above my rank and have me related by marriage to the Crown, linked by bonds other than those of just affection and confidence. Thus I saw myself, without much feting, single one night and married the next morning to petite María Teresa Borbón y Vallábriga, first cousin to the King, to Mayte with all her illnesses and fainting spells.[2]

But I was so alive and optimistic in those days that these complications did not hound me. At heart, I saw that, mistakenly, I wanted to take the lion's share: to enjoy at the same time Pepita's love, the prominence that my marriage meant to me, and the steady confidence of the King and Queen, into whose own domestic life in the palace I had naturally been drawn with the passing of the years. Miraculously, I had time and energies for everything: to fulfill my conjugal duties without giving Pepita up and, without sacrificing my personal life, to dedicate all my time to those things the King and Queen wanted me to do. All of that, working from sun up to sun down, at times until midnight in my office. Perhaps, simply, I had a certain talent for mixing duties and feelings, even if there were feelings among them that seemed irreconcilable. That epoch was portentous, turgid. And bitter in comparison with this exile and this decadence, this solitude and this abandonment, these current punishments.[3]

But I go back again fifty years to that animated and enjoyable 1797, to my Spain and my youth. In the pleasant routine at the palace, only one shadow was cast: Fernando, the firstborn, turned out to be a listless and apprehensive child who grew into a suspicious and sullen adolescent. He showed increasing indifference toward his parents and even certain mistrust and hostility. The love Their Majesties showed him, every day more distressed and eager, did not seem to conquer that resistance, but it increased it, nor did their expressions of love serve any purpose other than to move him to rebuffs and disdain. Don Carlos was offended and pained; Doña María Luisa, her suffering worse because of her female intuition, foresaw the gravity of the problem, if not the exact disaster, for the family as well as the nation, which this would all lead to ten years later.[4]

For a time, coinciding with Fernando's first signs of puberty, which to be honest was developing unpleasantly, everyone was consoled a bit because the boy, while pulling away from his parents, was showing signs of a growing fondness toward me, as if I were, in the awakening of his virility, the model he would have chosen, more by an impulse of youthful desires than by a thought-out plan. So at times, even with a certain insistence and exaggeration, Fernando sought my company, took pleasure asking endless questions and encouraging me to tell stories, imitated my walk and my way of dressing, and even tried to meddle in my work or sneak away to my side at the stables, in my dressing room, at the pelota courts, or at the casino, as if an apprenticeship in the masculine world had been added to complement the pious teaching of his tutor, the priest Escóiquiz. His august parents felt unconditional appreciation toward me. They came to see the Prince's favor as a kind of compensation for his conspicuous rejection of them. Until suddenly—at the time, I assumed on account of some inadvertent, stupid act of mine, but today I know beyond a shadow of a doubt that it was because of Escóiquiz's malicious influence—one day Fernando stopped looking for me, imitating me, even talking to me. He made me the obvious victim of a loathing much more visible than what he showed toward his parents. The King and Queen felt saddened; I preferred to suffer in silence, in hopes that those changes and oppositions of an adolescent whim would pass.[5]

Those unsettling events did not affect my old friendship with the Queen; rather they fortified it. That friendship was really so solid, so unshakable on its foundations and in its active and permanent support. I understand how outsiders' eyes can find it difficult to imagine the friendship as it survived all the tragic vicissitudes it was exposed to for more than six lustrums, remaining undamaged even to my eminent friend's last breath, exhaled at the end of her final vows of loyalty and gratitude toward me.[6] Less dramatic, although also singular and perhaps more significant, is that during the period of time to which I am referring, I overcame also the pitfall that could be attributed to my whims: Pepita's appearance in my life and the quickness with which I accepted their marrying me off to Mayte. Doña María Luisa was a woman, while passionate, also exceptionally sensible and understanding. She learned to safeguard the singularity and depth of our affection in all apparently adverse circumstances. She was, in addition to all ties, including the sacred bond that united the patron to her favorite, a friend and a mother. I want these words to stand as homage to that unbreakable affection, to that great woman who—I know—will find a way from her place with the Lord to understand once more and to forgive once more: what I see myself to be now, because of the obligation that I have imposed on myself to write this Memoir, as I refer to some of our intimacies.

My encounters with Doña María Luisa, apart from our daily and nearly constant meetings in the King's presence, took place in those chambers in the left wing of the palace that were always available for my repose any time of the day. Only my valet and I had the key to those rooms. He was assigned to have them clean and in order with changes of undergarments and fruit drinks and sweets I might want during the brief siestas I allowed myself on those very long, hard days. The Queen herself had her key, of course, and this, I suspect, was an open secret. But she did not use it at her will, only on prearranged days and times—Tuesdays and Fridays at six in the afternoon. The King, extremely methodical as he was, dedicated those afternoons every week of the year to his personal recreation: carpentry. Old Maestro Bertoldo, the renowned Italian craftsman who was in charge of the cabinetry work at the Casita del Labrador in Aranjuez,[7] came to the palace on those days and directed the King's projects in his workshop, which he had had built for that purpose. Even when the Court was not in Madrid, as happened many months of the year for long stretches of time, when the King was at La Granja, the Escorial, or in Aranjuez itself, Bertoldo would travel as one of the retinue, so addicted was His Majesty to his lessons and to his Tuesday/Friday diversion. So that if I also happened to be staying at any of those palaces, my rendezvous with Doña María Luisa were held the same as in Madrid, in the lodgings assigned to me wherever I was. Only one of us being ill, some diplomatic commitment that could not be postponed, or war itself would force us to suspend our meetings. But, in general, I should say that our good health, the ease with which the Queen put off the most arrogant ambassador, and the brevity of wars in those years made rare the Tuesdays and Fridays that did not allow our clandestine meetings.

And now, so the reader may completely understand that story, I have no choice but to explain what those meetings consisted of and in what atmosphere they unfolded.

There inside my chambers, we were no longer Your Majesty and Manuel. We were transformed by a magic avatar to just Malú and Manú, the affectionate nicknames of our secret intimacy, invented almost from the beginning. Reciprocal and nearly identical invocations brought us close together, one to another, identified us apart from all our differences, including gender. Malú and Manú were friends, brother and sister, partners, pals, chums, members of a secret club of two based on a logic constituted solely by us and for us, twins from a single egg, identical, inseparable, indistinguishable, interchangeable. In the room with the high ceiling, with the blinds closed, with a soft, gray light to enfold them and shelter their games. That's what they were, games. And I doubt that anyone would be able to understand or admit their essential innocence. Malú and Manú were born every Tuesday and Friday at six in the afternoon, when I turned the key in the door that had just closed behind me, the first sign of recognition and greeting, and went over to the vast, white bed, shaded by the lace canopy, where Malú was waiting, naked, expectant, and happy. And after the first romp, the pet names, the laughter, the use of a code invented, known, consecrated entirely by Malú and Manú, the question that began the great game finally came: "Whom does Malú want to visit her today?" A question that, although it was usually posed by Manú, Malú herself could have posed it if it was a languid or lazy day and she preferred that time not to go to the trouble of choosing the person who would visit her. It was none other than Manú under any one of the disguises kept in the antechamber; the choice, whether made by Malú or by Manú himself, determined of course who would pronounce the abracadabra.

The origin of the costumes went back twelve years. I was then captain of the guard for Don Carlos III. Dragged along by my brother Luis one Saturday of Carnival, I attended a masked ball that the then Prince and Princess of Asturias sponsored, in a more or less unofficial capacity, for people whom I still had not had the immeasurable honor of knowing. At a costume store for actors in the Lavapiés neighborhood, I had rented a troubadour costume, threadbare but made of rich scarlet velvet with long white silk stockings—which accented almost too much my strong calf muscles—and which came with a stage-prop lute. I went to the party like that, and it was there that, for the first time, my lady Doña María Luisa's watchful eyes got a look at me. She and Don Carlos had already honored my brother Luis with their patronage, and they noticed him joking around with me. Pretty soon, they called me over. That was not only the origin of the costumes but also the moment that marked the course of my life forever.[8] The Princess did not want to ever forget that first image she had had of me—the jerkin, the beret with the little black-green feather, the stockings, the lute—and she was amused telling me that my Royal Guard uniform was nothing more, in the end, than another disguise, the same as that one, and that someday she would discover which was the real Manuel, the juggler or the hussar, as she laughingly called me.

Three or four years later, with Carlos III dead by then and she, therefore Queen, I, as captain, accompanied Their Majesties one afternoon to the plaza to see the very famous Pepe Hillo bullfight. I whispered secretly into the sovereign's ear my admiration for the matador's appearance and for his rich *traje de luces.* Can you imagine my surprise when a few days later a messenger brought an exquisitely wrapped box to my room, from which, amazed and in wonder, I pulled out another *traje de luces* even more splendid than the bullfighter's I had envied, covered with rhinestones and mother-of-pearl with inlaid work of reds and pinks and blacks, a true jewel of exquisite workmanship, accompanied by a brief note that read: "For Manuel, secret matador, who will know how to stab the unruly heifer." The note had no signature, but the intention and timing of the present, not to mention its largess, bespoke the highest lineage. Around then, Manú and Malú were born.

The bullfighter's costume was just the first of a long

series. Not a saint's day or birthday passed without a new costume being added to my closet—now signed by Malú. With the same affectionate signature there arrived every spring, every summer, and every fall from Aranjuez, La Granja, or the Escorial, new creations with which Malú filled her leisure time, thanks to the polished art of her tailors and seamstresses, creations she sent to her Manú, tied as he almost always was to Madrid's extreme temperatures because of his duties of state. So that outfits upon outfits were adding up in my antechamber until they formed an extravagant body of characters on hangers in the armoires. To the bullfighter were added the gladiator and the sailor, the crusading knight and the sultan, the emperor and the abbot, the shepherd and the pirate, the captain of the infantry and the Knight Templar, the mandarin, the raja from India and the humble convent gardener, not counting the people whom mythology supplied, so that at times, in one entire year, some of those characters remained banished and bored in the armoires, waiting in vain for the honor of visiting Malú, who each time had her preference in mind when she answered the question: Whom does Malú want to visit her today? Except when she allowed me to ask the question myself, and I had the chance to dust off some passed-over acrobat or forgotten knight errant.

While I retired for a few minutes to the antechamber, the time it would take me to work my transformation, she was doing hers, which always was simpler and easier, because strangely, Malú hated the embellishments of costumes and ornamentation in intimacy, and she solved it all with a few elements: a scarf that, often with more help from the imagination than from deftness, became a tunic, habit, chlamys, the torn dress of a captive or a shipwrecked woman; some combs that became cow's horns, the crucifix held aloft by the martyred woman or Judith's dagger to complement my bullfighter, my gladiator, or my Holofernes; a necklace that was the rosary in the hands of a novice, shackles on Briseis's ankles, a necklace around a Moorish princess's throat.

Because in the end, that's what the game was all about. When Manú came back in the room, Malú would be waiting, ready to act out the corresponding character in the well-directed ceremonial play: If Manú was the fierce and cruel Süleyman, Malú was the trembling Christian captive. However, when Manú was the rude and fanatical crusader, he would find Malú changed into the lofty Moorish woman full of spite and loathing; the intrepid sailor would throw himself into the sea to rescue the chaste shipwrecked woman; the lecherous gardener surprised the ecstatic little nun among the roses; the executioner dragged the sinner to the flames; and the honorable shepherd remained enchanted by the sight of the sleeping princess; Jupiter-bull, with his hide and horns, raped Europa between his paws; and Daphne was paralyzed in a tree at the touch of Apollo's fingers; Achilles was the only one who did not know for certain whom he would find in his tent when he returned from battle—whether it was Patroclus or Briseis, depending on a single turn of Malú's whims.[9] And at the same time as the play was unfolding, the character's identity was absorbed, dissolved in a liturgy that in every case meant confronting an assault, Manú's violence and power with resistance and flight, fight, and intrigue—and even agony and death were Malú's privilege, be she slave, sorceress, or heifer. The game ended, the disguise abandoned on the floor or among the sheets along with change of fortune, Malú and Manú returned to their true identity, they went from one complicity to another, from frenzy to tenderness, from battle to conspiracy, from the sinful game to the innocent game. Because, my distant reader, it was always a game.

There is an episode that I believe throws a posthumous light as an epilogue on this story of Malú and Manú.

Twenty years later, Doña María, already very old, recalled for Italian guests during a party at the Barberini Palace, the good times of her Madrid Court. And suddenly to my surprise and the King's, she turned to me, saying, "Manuel, let's enlighten our noble Roman friends with a demonstration rather than with stories. Go dress in your old uniforms, model them for everyone here, so they can see how you were, my dear Manuel, and so they may see how our Court was and all that we were once . . ." And there was no way to refuse. I had to put on a half-dozen dress uniforms that still accompanied me into exile from my old posts and official offices. It had been over ten years since they had seen the light of day. I dressed in them in an antechamber and paraded in each one before the astonished eyes of the other guests, who in all their embarrassment uttered exclamations of amazement or admiration on seeing the luxury and the richness of the high-buttoned tunics, the epaulets and buckles, the plumed hats—not even the Napoleonic generals had been decked out so fastidiously. But those Italians did not understand what was really happening in that majestic salon in the Roman palace: Malú, revived, was evoking Manú, other outfits, and other late afternoons from that Don Manuel she subjected to ridicule in that strange parade. I did not get to all the uniforms. With the third or fourth one a tremor began to shake the Queen's body, and something you could not distinguish as laughter or sobbing turned into a stream of tears and fainting. She had to be taken to her chambers. The party ended with that. Malú had been reborn for a moment, struggling with her youthful ardor, with her uncontainable love for the game, with a flux of irrepressible life under the folds of that august old woman's skirt. It was a strange incident; we never spoke of it later.[10] But the last words that Doña María Luisa murmured in my ear (she could do nothing more, due to the desolation of her agony) some months later were: "Whom does Malú want to visit her today?" If Manú had known how to, he would have dressed as sweet Death in that heavy Roman twilight.

Let's go back to 1797. One afternoon, not a Tuesday or Friday, I went to my rooms to freshen up and rest a while. Closing the door I heard, to my great surprise, a muffled voice commanding from the bedroom, "Lock the door." I obeyed mechanically, asking myself which one of us, Doña María Luisa or I, had gotten confused about the day or for what other reason she had broken the old custom, paying me an unexpected visit. I went toward the bedroom. Two bare arms sticking out from the sheets in the shadows of my bed confirmed right away that there had been a mistake. I started to say, "Malú, what's going on?" But the words froze on my lips, and all of me, body and soul, was paralyzed before what I saw, not believing my eyes. Fernando, the Prince, was in Malú's place; he was looking at me, his bulging eyes half-closed, his thick mouth half-open, the lower lip fallen under his sharp, little gray teeth, the upper lip drawn back under his oversized nose, a caricature of a smile that mixed fear and mocking. "Your Highness . . . ," was all I could mumble. I felt a blazing fire come over my face, while my knees, out of control, grew weak, comprehending what was going on before my confused mind caught up to what was happening. Then that sardonic and ignoble mouth pronounced the irremedial: "I was waiting for you, Manú . . ."

I felt dizzy, I staggered, a nausea rose up my throat like another flame, my face and temples still burned. In the middle of the horrible confusion, I know I saw the Prince's leggings and clothes tossed and wadded up on the floor, next to the bed. I remembered that in the past weeks Malú had heard, more than once, a sound in the sitting room and had feared that a rat had gotten in. I do not know how long I stood there in that panic—Don Fernando's dull-witted smile and gaze, his body that I knew was naked under the sheets, his clothes piled on the Persian rug—while he asked me, with the insistence of a hammer beating in my temples and squeezing my throat until I nearly vomited. Had I really heard correctly, had he said "Manú" and not just "Manuel"? But in any case, what was he doing there, what? . . . The questions bloomed on my lips: "What brings Your Highness to my chambers? Isn't this your time to study with Father Escóiquiz?" He laughed his short, moist laugh, like a splatter. "Come on, Manuel," he said. "This is my first time to visit you. You should be a better host." I was barely managing to control the shaking in my legs and that nausea waving over me. I still did not understand; I had not come out of my confusion. I tried to add, with the heartiness of a final slap one gives a drowning person, "I would be very pleased to receive Your Highness, but some other time. Now, I should get back to my office. My secretaries will be getting worried, and the poor priest will be concerned about Your Highness, too . . ." I was talking too much, with no conviction, like someone begging a conjurer to be awakened from a bad dream. But Don Fernando's cold and malevolent look did not allow me a way out of my delirium; it brought me to the terrible reality of his presence there, in my bedroom, in my bed; as did his cold, metallic voice, when he interrupted me, "Let's not waste any time, Manuel, since all those people are already worried and waiting for us. I also want to play. Ask me." Something in my brain rose like a barrier not letting me understand the frightening meaning of the Prince's order. My voice muffled, I answered, submissive, inert, "What should I ask, Your Highness?" The Prince smiled again (I cannot say if that was a smile or a grimace) and taking what seemed like an interminable length of time, said, in a grotesque, vile, monstrous imitation of his mother, "Whom does Fenú want to visit him today?"

"Fenú" he had said. There was no escape. It was as if suddenly a jail cell had fallen all around me, sealing me in its bars, and at the same time a hand had grabbed me by my clothes and, with a single jerk, had exposed me, naked, vulnerable, disgraced, pitiable, terrified, to the whole world. A rush of nausea rose to my mouth, and I was trembling all over, from fear, from shame, from anger, begging the Divine that all this was a dream, a sinister and comic nightmare, but Don Fernando's voice, once again, was the implacable and disheartening embodiment of reality. He insisted, "Ask me. That's an order."

Suddenly my knees quit shaking, the flush and fiery sensation went away. I was left feeling cold and immobile, nearly rigid in the face of my vertigo. So that, interpreting my silence as disobedience, he continued, "Very well. As you wish, Manuel. I don't need your cooperation." And after tying the two corners of the sheet at his neck, as if improvising a tunic, he concluded with a lofty and defiant look in his eyes, "Fenú wants to receive Süleyman."

I hated that vile, scaly-skinned bastard. Like a drug that stimulates the runner in the middle of a race, my hate was fed an energy that allowed me to assume suddenly a certain authority, to threaten him with dragging him by his ears to his father and to denounce his perversion to Escóiquiz. Of course, at that point I had lost all good judgment, and the only thing I managed with my warnings was to hear again, and now longer, cascading, and pounding, that despicable laugh that no one had been able to cure him of. "You've lost your head, my good Manuel," he said. "The only one who can threaten here is me. You could take the whole story to the King, true, or to the Holy Father. But I don't like weak threats.

My father is such an imbecile that he just might end up absolving you, and Escóiquiz isn't as strong as you'd think. If you don't obey me, I will go directly to the Inquisition and denounce you both, you and that whore, my mother." And wielding a key that he took from between his legs, he added, "I won't give you two time to destroy this key that I stole from my mother's jewel box or all the costumes you keep in those armoires." And he lowered his voice suddenly until it was no more than a sickening whisper, "Let's go. Fenú wants to receive Süleyman. What other choice do you have, Manú? Killing me?"

He had guessed it. All I was thinking about was killing him, wiping him from the face of the earth, but he knew that I could not do it, that I was lost, in his power. There was only one way out: Süleyman.[11]

If those minutes in front of my bed were the most atrocious that I have ever spent in my life, the resignation with which I had armed myself while I was changing clothes in the antechamber was, I assure you, not a relief, because it was done in hatred and humiliation. I had fallen into a trap, and, as Don Fernando had so very well described it, there was no solution other than to prepare myself in the best way possible to play my role as Süleyman. With the bitterness, at least, of knowing beforehand that my nature would facilitate things, that Süleyman would visit Fenú, more out of repugnance than anything Fenú could do to provoke him. Thus Manú was finished off. And I feel a moral necessity to declare for honesty's sake that that was not the first time I had had carnal relations with a person of the same sex. When I was twelve, the confessor at the Badajoz Cathedral had initiated me into certain practices that gave me pleasures beyond measure and that he used to execute on his knees in the cathedral meeting room. Then, later, as captain of the guard, I couldn't have been more than eighteen, one drunken night I gave in to the temptation of the tender and very sweet body of a foreign companion.[12] But, with all respect due to a Prince, who later with things the way they came to be, flaunted the Crown of the country for nearly twenty years, Don Fernando seemed particularly repulsive to me, and I rebelled beforehand against my nature's indiscriminant response to mere stimulation of contact or imagination.

And, the things that went on there in the bedroom were as I had foreseen in the antechamber. For my part, a mere animal release, carried out with more haste than desire; on his part, only the sterile satisfaction of whim, of an evil curiosity. Don Fernando gathered up his clothes with a sullen air, got dressed carelessly in the darkest corner of the room, and before leaving, tossed the key on the bed. He then said, in a voice that seemed to have become more mechanical, still tense, "I will never come back to your room. I detest you. I will detest you until my dying day."

And that ended that. From that day, urged on by Escóiquiz, from whom I suppose he always hid Fenú's sordid adventure, he began to conspire against me, a long and patient work that culminated more than ten years later in Aranjuez and in Bayonne, but he was not satisfied with that. His hatred toward me, who in the end had done nothing but obey him, who could not please him now, pursued me till his death. Even afterward, his intrigues and persecutions caused great repercussions in my life.

The King and Queen, of course, never found out what had happened. It was not a problem for me to slip the key into Doña María Luisa's hand, saying that she had forgotten it on her last visit. The truth is, from that afternoon on, the game of disguises had become very painful for me, and some part of that feeling must have affected the Queen, too. One day she gave the excuse of a meeting, another day an illness. One day we quit playing, and the silk of the costumes began to rot in the armoires.

Being still almost a child, the Prince found it easy, with the treacherous wind of Escóiquiz blowing in his ear, to find ways to keep alive his rancor toward me or to distrust any of my schemes. Few weeks had passed since our encounter, when on the pretext of his fourteenth birthday, he begged his father to let him regularly attend meetings of the Council of State, as a way to become adept in the science of governing the country. The King, showing signs of his prudence once again, understood that at that point in the Prince's education, he was not skilled enough yet to take such a step and denied him permission. Don Fernando threw a fit of anger; he cried and howled so much that the whole palace heard him say that because of my own insatiable ambitions I had influenced the King's will, and so had managed to keep him out of the negotiations of state. The atmosphere remained so charged with ill feelings, that I urgently begged my lord to release me from my post and allow me to leave the Court for a while. It was a plea that I repeated with growing frequency, weary as I was of jealousies and intrigues. This time, the good King, perhaps hoping to dispel the rumors that his own son had circulated, accepted my resignation. So it was that I found myself finally and happily parted from power and all my official duties. When I returned to them two years later, without ever completely distancing myself from the Monarchs' friendship and favor, there had already formed around the Prince a true faction whose objectives were to ruin once and for all my political career and even something more grave: to dishonor and displace the Queen.

Some years later, in 1802, as I have recounted in my Memoirs, there was a strong confrontation between the Prince and me, regarding his planned marriage to the Princess María Antonia of Naples. I advised his father, the King, to postpone the wedding, considering that the Prince was not ready yet at his age (he was, though, eighteen by then), at the level of learning, which was meager despite efforts to improve it, or with the moral integrity to assume the responsibilities of the state of matrimony and the freedom that that state brought with it. I thought the Prince should first complete his education and then correct his backwardness by traveling for two or three years throughout Europe, something that in those days we called "our century's cleansing." The King and Queen confided my doubts to Caballero, asking his advice. The disloyal minister, who met with the Prince and his band often in the Prince's chambers, the scene of rumors and conspiracies against my government, did not waste any time passing those doubts along to the Prince. The result was Don Fernando's fury at my intercession, which he judged to be ill intended—even to the point of feeling his very rights to the throne challenged. His resentment toward me was now complete.[13] This time, curiously, the Queen did not agree with me; she urged the King to marry the Prince off, because at the same time, through the same negotiations, the young Infanta, Isabel, was marrying María Antonia's brother, who had became King of Naples and the Two Sicilies, thus giving a new throne to the family. So the date for the double wedding was set against my advice, but that did not soothe Don Fernando's wrath. This aggravated matters, which of course affected the plotting in Don Fernando's chambers, which as I have already said, the Duchess of Alba herself frequented, halfway through July 1802 . . .

Notes

1. Although Godoy passes over the topic quickly, we should remember that at the death of the Duchess of Alba, and with the Monarchs' consent, he arranged for the City Hall of Madrid itself to acquire for him the Buenavista Palace; he had no great scruples in moving into the place where his ex-friend and lover had died tragically. In the same way, the Queen made a game of her privilege in order to buy the Duchess's jewels at a lower price, after trying unsuccessfully to seize them for herself with a Royal Order. Godoy learned how to keep for himself the better part of her works of art (*Toilet of Venus* by Velázquez, *Mercury Instructing Cupid* by Correggio, a Virgin by Raphael, among others) and even her servants, as is recorded in documents of the day.
2. The general opinion among historians is that María Luisa hurried along Godoy's marriage in order to neutralize his dangerous passion for Pepita Tudó. Godoy himself, in his Memoirs, briefly reports that Carlos IV "joined me to his family with the plan of elevating me to such a height where their fire could not reach me (that of his political enemies)." And he continues: "This tie was a work of his absolute will, not from some other means as my entrance to the ministry had been. Carlos IV ordered it in such a way that he left no time between the celebration of the marriage and the communication of his decree to the Council of State. I obeyed him in this matter loyally and submissively as I did in all the other acts of my life." And a little further on he says in the only reference to Pepita and to the rumors that were circulating about a previous marriage to her: "Time has done justice to the base calumny that they (enemies and envy) promoted, revealing that I broke other sacred vows in order to celebrate this marriage." In any case, it is clear

that María Teresa de Borbón y Vallábriga was sacrificied at sixteen years old to the "reason of state" or to the sentimental interests of the Queen and to a disinterested husband, who was doing nothing more than obeying a royal decision.

3. Since 1848, Godoy evokes with nostalgia his golden age. In 1819, the Monarchs had died, and in 1835 Pepita left him alone in Paris in order to conduct personally his unending litigations in Madrid and never returned to his side. At this point, Godoy is nothing more than the eccentric (and of course mythomaniac) "Monsieur Manuel," who sits on a bench in the Palais Royal to get some sun and tells his skeptical little friends, very young children, stories of old battles and forgotten glories. But it is very likely that in that solitude Godoy tends to idealize his youthful capacity to mix work and love. Although testimony from that period vouches for his exceptional dedication to government duties, this is also what Jovellanos himself wrote about in his diary of November 22, 1797, his moral repugnance concerning the indifference with which Godoy faced and exhibited his amorous life: "The Prince invites us to eat at his house. To his right, the Princess; to his left, close by his side, that Pepita Tudó . . . This spectacle caused my confusion; my soul cannot suffer him; I did not eat, or talk, nor could I calm my spirit; I fled from there, stayed at home all afternoon, uneasy and disheartened, wanting to do something and wasting time and my thoughts." If this text has merit in giving an idea of Jovellanos's extreme puritanism, it also has merit to judge that "art" Godoy attributes to himself to be able to mix affections, "although they seem irreconcilable."

4. The 1808 mutiny in Aranjuez against Godoy. Bayonne. The fall of the Bourbons. The Napoleonic invasion. The war.

5. Today it is thoroughly documented that young Fernando did have a natural propensity to mistrust and to

somber pondering, to which is added the malevolent influence of the curate Escóiquiz, whom, paradoxically, Godoy himself had chosen some years before as the Prince's precept.

6. Godoy is not exaggerating. The Duchess of Luca, once Queen of Etruria, daughter of Carlos IV and María Luisa, said to her brother Fernando VII a little while after her mother's death: "The day before she died, she called me to her bed and said to me, 'I am dying. I recommend Manuel to you. You can have him, you and your brother Fernando, and you can be sure that there is no one more affectionate.' I kissed her hand. I told her that I loved her with all my soul. That was the last time that I could talk to her . . ."

7. Another error Godoy's memory commits. The Casita del Labrador was not built until much later, into the nineteenth century, although certainly by Carlos IV and María Luisa.

8. The version that Godoy gives of that first meeting with the Prince and Princess of Asturias dispels a myth and also explains, in part, another. According to one version, which now seems totally false, Carlos and María Luisa noticed him for the first time because of a bucking mount and the bravery the young Manuel demonstrated with his horse. In another legendary version, the thing that got the Prince and Princess's attention was his singing accompanied by a guitar. This would seem to be an extrapolation of this original situation: the costume of the juggler and the stage-prop lute.

9. Aside from denoting a level of classical culture that today would seem estimable and surprising in two people that posterity has not judged as particularly cultivated, the inspiration of the "dramas" put on by Manú and Malú calls attention to European literature of the end of the eighteenth century and the beginning of the nineteenth. The fiery Turk and his Christian captive, or its opposite, the crusader and the Moorish woman, inevi-

tably call to mind Lord Byron; the shy, shipwrecked woman and the sailor seem a depiction of the end of *Paul et Virginie* by Bernardin de St. Pierre; the executioner and the sorceress evoke violent images from the Gothic English novel; the gardener and the nun breathe the sacrilegious air of certain French romanticism. Before imagining María Luisa or Godoy avid readers of the latest publications, one has to think that the writers molded a mythology that was populated by the imagination of society before being shaped into books.

10. Bausset refers to the episode with the uniforms in the Barberini Palace in his *Mémoires anecdotiques sur l'intérieur du palais impérial*, the difference being that Godoy situates it closer to the Queen's death and Bausset several years before.

11. If we suppose that the incident that Godoy recounts was warped by his resentment toward Fernando VII, it is interesting to compare it with another, publicly and historically documented, which occurred in 1814 on the occasion of Fernando's trip from Valençay to Valencia at his rise as Constitutional Monarch of Spain. His antagonist, on that occasion, was coincidentally Godoy's brother-in-law, Cardinal Luis de Borbón, then president of the Constitutional Regency, who was also traveling to Levante to get Fernando's pledge. The respective retinues of Fernando and the Cardinal encountered each other in Puzol, eighteen kilometers northeast of Valencia. The two central figures got down from their carriages. Each one stood waiting for the other to leave the encounter. The Cardinal, finally, chose to advance, and Fernando, since he was King, extended his hand so that the Cardinal could kiss it. But Fernando still had not sworn allegiance to the Constitution and could not be recognized as King yet, so that the Cardinal, naturally, vacillated. Fernando, after a moment, his face red with anger according to witnesses, raised his hand toward the Cardinal's nose and ordered: "Kiss it." The Cardinal

bowed and kissed it. Doesn't that "Kiss it" seem amazingly to parallel, with aspects of whim, arbitrary acts, and abuse of power, the Prince's words to Godoy in the bedroom, as a result of circumstances more diverse than they would seem to be?

12. In chapter 2 of his Memoirs, after narrating his admission into the body of Carlos III's guard, Godoy says: "There I have two companions who are brothers, last name Joubert, born in France, educated in that country, highly trained, studious without measure, both of them with the sweetest habits, with both of whom I joined in ties of friendship, that lineage of true and generous friendship that is engendered at the youthful age." Interesting the repetition of the adjective "sweetest" so many years later. Could it be too bold to think that one of the Jouberts is the "foreign companion" that Godoy was referring to?

13. The complete story of Godoy's frustrated intervention with Carlos IV to gain the postponement of the wedding can be read in chapter 11 of the second part of his Memoirs. There he likewise says that the weddings were set for April 14, 1802.

MY STORY

II

THAT summer I was in La Granja with the Court. More and more, the King and Queen insisted on having me at their side, as if being physically close to each other were more important for guiding the ship of state than my presence in Madrid, confronting the government and the ministers. I always gave in, counting on initiatives and intrigues of diplomacy, worries and petitions from the people being tabled due to their habit of taking a respite in the summer's heat. The Queen, now that our games on Tuesdays and Fridays remained buried, if not forgotten, forever in the past, seemed more and more eager to have my company, as if we could, by sitting face-to-face with a deck of cards, exorcise the dangers that her keen intuition saw hovering over Spain, over the Crown, and over her own family; dangers that she clearly attributed entirely to the Prince's personality, to the ant-like activity of his coterie of accomplices or instigators, and to the swollen river of murmurings and calumny that flowed unceasingly from his chambers in the palace. That summer, the Prince had not wanted to move from Madrid, claiming there were some studies he wanted to finish before getting married and which we all knew did not exist. That, on top of other things, should have warned me not to go on vacation to La Granja, but the Queen insisted, hounded the King, arguing that they had given him the fervor and the authority. So, I ended up there, idling away the hours among the gardens and the fountains during the day and playing endless games of *crapaud* at night, face-to-face with Doña María Luisa, who, as I say, while she had me at her side and could rub my knee like a talisman, breathed easier for the nation's fortune and for her own.

In mid-July, I got a letter along with my private correspondence that said simply, "Colombina returned to her home after her last escapade, Arlecchino courts her again, Captain Fracassa has left his tent, and the three have set about to study the "fabric" of a new comic intermezzo. Wouldn't it be prudent for you to give it a reading before the premiere? Il Suggeritore." The letter was a clear warning. While I had lost time in La Granja, my enemies had gained it in Madrid. The Duchess (Colombina) had returned from Andalucía, she was meeting Fernando (Arlecchino) and Cornel (the Captain). The three were embroiled in some new intrigue involving Italy and very probably the King of Naples. The code, in that sense, was wrong: the masks of the *commedia dell'arte* changed names according to the nationality of the persons who held the strings from the opposite end of the plot. If they had been French, for example, Arlecchino would have been renamed Sganarelle. Besides the forthcoming double wedding, the sting that still remained from my intervention to get the King to postpone the date and the Neapolitan Court's old grudge toward our French politics amply guaranteed the possibility of some maneuver the enemies under our roof would embark upon in the middle of summer. That very night, I showed the letter to the King and Queen. Doña María Luisa did not hide her resistance but admitted that I should return to Madrid, especially since my correspondent had explicitly promised in the last sentence to place in my hands the secret documents concerning what our "players" were up to. So, at dawn I got on the road.

I did not go home when I arrived in Madrid but went directly to the royal palace. I still had my private rooms there, I had ample change of clothes, and I promised myself, while I was waiting to get in touch with the author of the letter, to spend at least one night in Pepita's company, without unnecessarily bothering Mayte, whose silences charged with dark resentment had become increasingly more unbearable. I took care of some matters in the palace, sent word of my arrival to Pepita and, in the afternoon, I decided to pay a visit to Goya's studio. The truth is that I was going not just to check on the progress of my "nude" but also to talk with Don Fancho about a new equestrian portrait, which Doña María Luisa had persuaded me at La Granja to have commissioned. I did not manage to settle that second purpose on my visit that afternoon; the turn of events forced me to postpone it and later Goya, citing vague health problems, flatly refused to do the portrait for me.[14]

I should say again that the meeting with Cayetana was totally accidental; it was not arranged beforehand as Goya's jealous suspicions lead him to believe. Nevertheless, it was a fortunate and at the same time fortuitous encounter as will be understood immediately. Cayetana said those daring words that I suppose Goya managed to hear: "You can come with any one of your wives . . ." Right away, with the prudence that the circumstances advised, she turned her back to the Maestro, lowered her voice, and continued quickly: "I'm glad you've returned," she said. "The matter warrants it. Come tonight and we'll find a moment so that I can show you those papers. But be careful. Fernando and Cornel are also invited."

I can imagine my readers' astonishment and scandal. Cayetana de Alba was working for the group she pretended to combat. And I should again go back to the past to explain how we had come to this curious situation: an old lover, through chance and after having first been a political enemy, later became an ally, an accomplice, and to use a word that Cayetana certainly was not frightened by at all, rather one she delighted in calling herself: a spy.

Since my days as an officer, the image of the young Duchess of Alba—with her amazing cascade of black curls, elegant, with a happy and festive disposition, and with a reputation of being a free thinker and a tiny bit licentious—disturbed the waking hours and the dreams of the entire corps of the guard and, in particular, mine. But, despite her celebrated simplicity, she was, because of rank and status, like a distant planet, inaccessible, the private property of a grandee of Spain, and in the majority of cases, of her equals. Those were also the years when the rivalry between the Duchess with the Princess of Asturias herself arose actively and frivolously. So many and so often were the excuses for competition—dresses and jewels, parties and tournaments, suitors and protégés—it may have been an unpardonable error on my part to show signs of the slightest interest in the Duchess, when the Princess was so openly jealous of her. A high price, given that I risked losing something secure even for the sake of such a tempting, distant, and aloof prize.[15]

It turned out that, ten years later, I had also acquired greatness by my methods and means; that the fickle little Duchess had been transformed into a capable and splendid woman. We two found ourselves one afternoon in 1794 in my office—I was by then first secretary of state. She was soliciting my patronage for a charity ball that she was organizing on the San Isidro greens. We felt, on being alone for the first time, that destiny had placed a challenge before us and that we would not be living up to our standards, neither of us, if we did not accept it. I want to say that there had never been between us a prologue of love nor pretense of love, except a chance recognition of being confronted by an unmatched rival of the opposite sex. We felt obliged to accept the challenge even if it only united us carnally. We were like two magnificent duelists, condemned to battle each other, two horses competing in a race that rules out vain comparison of their prowess, the piano and the violin, getting to the heart of the sonata's secret and emulating it implacably. It may seem extreme pride on my part, and certainly I would not have confessed it then; but at eighty years old, reduced as I am to waiting for death, well I can say that at twenty-six I was the most handsome—and most sought after—man at Court, the only one who could stare Cayetana de Alba in the eye and tell her with a look: you are the first among females, and I recognize no rival among males.[16] So, a little while after that encounter, we became lovers, admitting we were fatally drawn to it. Equal to equal, without courtship or seduction, resistance or pressure, enticement or bargaining on either part to get in the way, free of anything that was not our own contest, that of our sexes, of that that made us as nothing else could, equals.

I insist that there was nothing amorously sentimental, nor any pretext of it. That, I believe, that sense of freedom without cost, was the trap we set for ourselves, because the next day, exalted, we came looking for each other, and the next day too, and an inexhaustible spring followed. It was abruptly curtailed before we could analyze what had happened, when our imprudence tickled the Queen's ears. That little breeze did not take long to grow to a hurricane destroying everything in its path: I was accused of betrayal and was threatened with losing all favors and with the scandal, which would have involved the Duchess, too. Lying a bit, covering up another part, and sincerely repenting the rest, I managed to get the river back in its banks. But Doña María Luisa was aware of having corrected a grave danger and she knew—she was still young then—how to drive out all danger of its happening again. Cayetana and I did not see each other again for many years.[17]

In the meantime, I met Pepita, fell in love with her, and married Mayte; it is not a bitter irony, or if it is, it was destiny that embraced us three. Cayetana, widowed, had dedicated herself to having lovers beneath her rank—a painter, Goya; a bullfighter or two, Costillares, Pepe Hillo, perhaps?; an actor whose name I have forgotten. Over time, perhaps out of spite, although it is not a sentiment that you naturally associate with her, she began to frequent Don Fernando's room and to join the ranks of his political band, against the Queen and me. Around 1800, we got together again. We repeated the passion, but not the wonder. She was greatly changed, distrusting, insecure; I sensed it even in her way of looking at me, with suspicion under her very long eyelashes, as if she wanted to control the unfortunate reflection of the years in my eyes.[18] She confessed she was annoyed, bored with everything, with men and politics. She said she was looking for other stimulation in life. And so, we came up with our extraordinary pact. If she had such a poor impression of the Prince, if all his schemes ended up seeming like petty kitchen gossip to her, in the end, if she saw no project, no perspective, no progress for Spain in the political artifice she continued to be involved in out of ennui, she certainly could switch from that group without saying so—the idea was hers, not mine—and to begin to work for me, someone who was already a known quantity, despite the disdain the King had inspired in her and the animosity that she already felt for the Queen. I was a man of state who could bring the nation to a more secure port than the fainthearted Don Fernando and his perverse cabal.[19] It all began as a joke that afternoon in her bed in the Moncloa Palace, but two days later a bulging envelope arrived at my office containing extremelv interesting reports about the correspondence and the ties that Father Escóiquiz had managed to piece together with the papal ambassador. We began to get together, again, in secret; but now it was to coordinate our codes, for her to inform me of what had gone on that evening in the Prince's chambers, or for me to ask her to investigate this or that. We rarely had sex. We were two conspirators, not lovers.

Even when I had shrugged off the last part of that party, without a doubt the most painful—Cayetana, torch in hand, making a fool of herself in front of everyone, the party closing on a lugubrious note—I must say that her uneasiness that night never took a breather, and while I certainly agree with Goya in giving Cayetana credit for her most exquisite talents as a hostess, that was not one of the times when they shone the most. For me, they were many, very strained hours rewarded only by the reading of the document that, at one point, she was able to put in my hands.[20] Truth is, those hours amassed all sorts of mishaps. First there was Cayetana's carelessness to invite me "with any one of my wives" and the unexpected, for me at least, arrival of Mayte with her brother. We all had to resort to worldly distraction to overlook that annoyance, Mayte, Pepita, and me above all, who were affected the most by something that, without being so exactly, had appeared to be deceit unfortunately discovered. I knew that I need not expect a single reproach from Mayte, but rather a greater thicket of suffocating silence around the house. As for Pepita, she always knew how to exercise patience and keep herself on another plane; to expose her unnecessarily to such controversy was to aggravate her too much in an unjust way. We had barely managed to rise above this embarrassment when the Count of Haro made an unfortunate allusion to the Prince's upcoming wedding, a thorny theme if ever there was one to be discussed in his presence and mine.

Don Fernando, who never missed an opportunity to attack, especially in public, hissed to the imprudent Count, who was congratulating him, "Yes, I am getting married in September, to the dismay of some who have wanted once more to put their ambitions before my happiness." His words like a slap, I did not take up the gauntlet. My only comment was, "Their Majesties have decided to make these weddings a true national celebration." To which the Prince responded flippantly, "Are they, Manuel?" And my reply, "The greatest since your birth, Highness."[21] In that moment of extreme tension, the Duchess came in, followed by Goya and Pignatelli, and I remember she came in laughing, which helped to clear the air. But after only one hour, I had figured in two incidents of ill feelings that could not be masked. Finally, during the meal, Cayetana's daring rose, stirring up antagonism that we could take lightly when she dealt with the Osuna woman or Costillares, but when she brought up her current relationship with me and with the Queen, she was treading on much rougher terrain. The Prince did not miss the chance to be disagreeable once more. I thought I even caught a glimpse of suspicion, as if he feared Cayetana was not playing straight with him, in a word as if he were on the verge of figuring out the truth. "Don't be afraid of the Duchess, Manuel," he said to me across the table. "She usually takes your part and defends you in my chambers." And he added, turning to Cayetana: "I hope you do the same for me, dear, when someone is talking about me in Sr. Godoy's chambers." He seemed, in some way to be referring to Cayetana's double game, but she did not respond to the allusion and continued the bold inquisition of her enemies. The Prince was not in the mood to be quiet, and he went on to the owner of the house, "You can rest easy. Godoy could not have burned the palace, Cayetana, since he wasn't sure I was inside. Now I see why you have invited him at the last moment. So, he won't set us on fire." And he laughed his horrible laugh, making everyone uncomfortable; only Goya's deafness—natural? voluntary?—saved him from experiencing that moment. A minute later, the Prince found a chance to refer to the old rivalry between Cayetana and his mother, and he had no misgivings about grossly pointing out Pignatelli with his knife (and with his tongue): "Before, you two only fought over young dandies and things were smoothed over by an exiling of the person in question. But now, dear Cayetana, what is at stake is Spain, and we can not send her to Paris while you two calm your nerves." I have always remembered the Prince's imprudent joke (which few graced with a little embarrassed laugh) as a dark prophecy of the events that, six years later and through his faction's ominous workings, ended in some way with Spain's fortunes bound and surrendered to France. But no one was thinking about that that night, not even the Prince. Everyone else, I suppose, abhorred above all his language and remembered wistfully the days when the Prince was quiet and did not say much. Because if he had learned one thing over the years it was how to start a true social calamity.[22]

The walk by torchlight was a slow current; the conversation became dispersed and light, the jealous Prince finally quieted down, and Cayetana, for a while, paid more attention to making the party agreeable to her guests than to trying out new, upsetting games. She had said to me, nevertheless, that afternoon in Goya's studio, that she would find a moment to show me those papers. The moment had not presented itself, and we were already well into the night. As if to quiet my impatience, she glided to my side while we were listening to the Boccherini trio and said, "When we all go downstairs, amuse yourself here upstairs and wait for me in my suite."

The discussion of the poisons and Mayte's fainting facilitated things. When we left my wife and my brother-in-law in Goya's workshop and everyone went to the hall of mirrors, I walked to the first floor. It was very easy for me to pretend to still be preoccupied with Mayte and linger around the door until everyone had disappeared down the corridor. In the dramatic light of a torch held by a servant left behind to light our way, poor Mayte, her eyes closed, rested her fragile little head and long neck on the purple clad shoulder of her older brother, who embraced her tenderly. It was a picture of abandon and tenderness, but I could not stop to contemplate it.

I ran to Cayetana's chambers through the solitary and ghostly parlor. I knew where it was from two previous visits, made at the edge of dawn and when Cayetana still was not completely settled in the palace. I was happy to find the rooms furnished and lit, and I settled down to wait. But it wasn't easy for me. It's never easy to wait in a woman's room. In this way, without her there, it's an unknown world where you're afraid to move, sit, smoke, or read. I don't mean it's a hostile world, but foreign, desolate, where we men feel at the same time intruders and trapped. I wished Cayetana would appear as soon as possible. Then, I saw the glass. I had never seen it before. It was such a magnificent piece, and it reflected the soft and fluctuating candlelight in such a way that it made me forget my impatience and my bad feelings. I picked it up, admired its smalts, the lady with her hair piled high, the stag with the tall antlers, the amazing turquoise and gold arabesque. I ran the end of my finger over its delicate edge; I tried to make the crystal sing with my nail.[23] I pricked up my ear and heard footsteps. I set down the glass and went toward the door that I had left open. Cayetana arrived and we stopped there a moment. I wrapped her in my arms, kissed her. It had been a long time since I had seen her so captivating. (I was not aware that I was really kissing Goya's last portrait of her.) In the silence we heard another noise. Cayetana looked in the parlor's mirrors. "Your wife. Your brother-in-law. And Goya," she murmured, and we closed the door. We were alone. And out of danger of any indiscretion, we believed.

The room recovered its order, its feeling, just by having a woman there. Cayetana went to the dresser, corrected the glass's position, as if she had guessed I had just touched it. And then she looked for a long time in the mirror. "My God!" she exclaimed. "What a maja I am tonight!" It was an adjective she liked to apply to herself, but this time she said it without a trace of humor, like a line in a play. I smiled, wrapped my arms around her waist again and kissed her neck. "Don't kiss me there," she mumbled. "You'll be poisoned." I did not understand what she meant; I did not know the whole story. But it was not the time to ask questions. "We should hurry," she said. "Let's not be gone long." She pulled away from me, laughed, walked to her bedroom. "Which of your wives is the most jealous?" she teased. "The one in La Granja, I bet." I did not answer; I sat on the stool in front of the dresser, my back to the candlelight and waited for her to show me the papers. When she came back, she had them in her hand. There were four or five sheets written with very narrow, tall handwriting, Don Fernando's. They were addressed to his future mother-in-law, the Queen of Naples. Even the opening was typical of him: "My dear and only mother," most reprehensible because of the way it implied a rejection of his true progenitress. The tone of adulation did not vary throughout the letter, that, above all, was a detailed and exhaustive rundown of our latest strategies agreed upon vis-à-vis France and England; a secret of state that should have been guarded not only by the Prince of Asturias but also by any honorable Spaniard.[24] But the Prince was not just any Spaniard; he was a vile Spaniard, rancorous, plotting, ready to carry his country to catastrophe, as he did later, to satisfy his malevolence and his rancor toward his parents and toward me. Those good people, torn between loving him as a son and suspecting him as their enemy, did not ever stop lavishing on him their confidence in the matters of state, even to the last. What he did not learn from them or from his ignoble acts of espionage, he learned from the minister Caballero, who was more an accomplice of his than a collaborator of ours, although good-hearted Don Carlos IV never stopped believing in him. Here was the proof, this detailed letter, that tied the long-winded accusations to twisted malice and the invention of calumny, a letter that he put in the hands of the Bourbons of Naples, and through their Court, in Metternich and Pitt's. That could only result in our greater isolation and vulnerability before the French Emperor.[25] While I was reading, I forgot all about Cayetana, who had stretched out on a divan, in front of me, and was playing with the fringe of her cashmere shawl, her eyes glued to mine, waiting for signs of my anger as the best reward for her good work. "How did you get a hold of this?" I asked. "It's only a copy," was her answer. "The original has already left for Naples. But it is my job to translate it into French and English, because the Prince can't do it."[26] "Then, the plan is for it to go to England and get to the French realists," I said. "Do you know who his correspondents are?" "No. But I'll find out," Cayetana assured me, not getting up from her graceful pose of abandon. "Since I can't translate all the flattery and trifling words he says to his mother-in-law, and because I must substitute something for them, I'll have to know who . . ." Just then, we heard the first noise.

It was just a rustling, a little creak that could come from a footstep or a body leaning involuntarily against the door, but it could have just been the groan of inanimate material in the silence of the night. Cayetana jumped to her feet right away. I instinctively hid the sheets of paper under my tunic. She said, "Something to drink? I have here a very fine sherry that they just gave me in Sanlúcar. I keep it in my room, for special guests . . ." I understood right away the game she was playing. If someone was listening, he should believe that this was an amorous interlude; if they had not already irreparably heard, as I feared, a part of our conversation about the letter. But now we had to go on playing the game. "I don't feel like drinking anything right now," I answered, taking her by the arm and stopping her from filling the two glasses on the little side table that held two or three bottles. "Kiss me." She obeyed. We kissed. Under my breath, I whispered very softly, "What do I do with the letter?" and she answered with barely a breath: "I've made a copy. I'll give it to you right now." We kissed again, all our attention poised on that thick silence that seemed to surround us, like a net, and behind which, in the background, you could hear the trio playing something by Haydn. Although nothing had been said that would inform any listener, we had to go on pretending. Embracing her still, I handed her the letter, and she disappeared again into the bedroom to exchange it for another. As if our own silence were a confession of guilt, I felt compelled to say something, and in that moment my eyes fell on the Venetian glass again. "All right, I'll have some wine," I said in a loud voice, "on the condition that I can drink it in that turquoise-colored glass." "You have good taste," Cayetana said, returning. "It's a collector's piece." "I imagine so. It's the most beautiful glass I've ever seen," I agreed, taking the letter. "And I'm bent on drinking from it as proof I'm not immune to your charms." At this point, it seemed that the letter and the glass were one, and that drinking was the code that was translated by reading that letter, keeping it, or taking it. It was no code; it was the irrational association that was born of our interruption. Cayetana filled the glass with sherry and handed it to me. "Drink up, then." I drank a sip. "I want to try it too," she purred, insinuatingly. I put the glass down. I embraced her again and passed the wine from my mouth to hers, imagining in my folly that those silent passes that one could only guess at from behind the door, would drive any idea of what he had really surprised us at from the spy's mind. But at the same time, unmistakably, I felt Cayetana becoming more and more desirable with the wooing meant for the invisible witness. "Let's leave the rest of it here. I'll drink afterward to celebrate getting reacquainted," I added. "Now I want to have you in my arms. Let's go to your bedroom." It was no longer a play. "Let's go," Cayetana repeated like an echo. "It doesn't matter anymore if they miss us. That goose of a Prince has no idea that you really are setting my palace on fire." Cayetana was not pretending either.

Wrapped in each other's arms, caressing each other, we had already turned to go to her bedroom, when we heard the second noise. First a dull thud and then a rapid, scraping noise in decrescendo, like footsteps going away. There was no doubt about it this time. Someone had been listening behind the door. In the face of certainty, it was better to make sure. I went stealthily down the back hallway. There was no one. The hall of mirrors was empty and silent. But a shadow crossed the vein of light coming from the open door to Goya's workshop. Nevertheless, when I looked in the mirror that had reflected that shadow, drawn by the movement, my eyes got there too late; the shadow had already disappeared, and there was nothing more than the luminous vein, quiet and enigmatic. For a moment I thought about Goya, but his thick peasant body could not have slipped away over the marble in the salon at that speed. Nevertheless, I was sure the spy was still there, hidden in Goya's workshop, since there was no other way out. I could have just gone over and exposed him. Who, I wondered, was going to expose whom? I hesitated; just then, my left foot tripped over something. I leaned over to pick it up. It was a small object, soft to the touch, that fit in the curve of my palm. I raised it to the light, coming from Cayetana's room. It was a small and very fine little sack made of kid leather, branded with the Asturias arms, and inside there was a little flask of smelling salts belonging to Don Fernando. I had seen my brother-in-law return it to the Prince after he offered them with annoying solicitude to help Mayte. It was Don Fernando, then, who had been listening outside the door. But what had he heard? Only our amorous play about the glass and the wine? Or something that at this very moment proved to him that Cayetana was my ally and not his? He would be furious, hidden there, frightened, close to having one of his attacks. (Those he could only remedy with the salts and that no one had ever wanted to call epilepsy).[27] What should I do? I made a quick decision. I kept the flask of salts and decided not to say anything to Cayetana for the moment. I would tell her for now that the wind must have made that noise, an open window in the hall of mirrors, a curtain blowing. Right now, I wanted above all to have her in my arms. She dropped her arms, and the fire-colored dress glided all the way down her body, until it rested like a giant rose on the pillow.

When I went downstairs, letting Cayetana go ahead a few minutes, I crossed the long hall of mirrors in the shadows and I saw Goya, distracted, seated in front of the window in his workshop. His presence confirmed, if it had really been necessary, that he had not been the spy. I could have gone in and asked him whom he had seen a half hour before, but I knew his answer: the name of the owner of the little rock crystal vial with lapis lazuli stopper that I had in my pocket. I dismissed the question and hurried on downstairs. In the vestibule I ran into my brother-in-law, Don Luis, who was coming from a visit to the palace oratory in the company of Cayetana's chaplain. Now in the parlor, I turned directly to Don Fernando and held out the little kid skin sack in my open palm. "I believe this is yours, Highness," was all I said. He practically grabbed it from me, not holding his anger in. No one had seen us. We had another secret to share. This time it was that he liked to slip down hallways and look into other people's bedrooms.[28] At that point, I nearly rejected the idea that he had heard the first part of our conversation.

I did not stay at the palace much longer. Mayte began to feel sick again, and I could not avoid offering her my companionship. We went home in silence. That silence arising from her vague resentment, incapable of materializing in reproaches or shouts. Perhaps she did not forgive me for surprising her in Madrid and in Pepita's company; perhaps she had figured out that I had been absent an hour during the party. Perhaps. I do not know. With her, you never knew. She had opted for silence.[29]

Notes

14. We already know that. Goya refused to paint after the Duchess's death. Nevertheless, in his letter to Zapater concerning the Duchess's makeup, Goya alludes to the commission for an equestrian portrait, which means that Godoy had arranged to commission him.

15. Pignatelli, whom Goya mentions so often in his story, was himself the object of a famous rivalry between the Duchess and the then Princess of Asturias. Ramón Gómez de la Serna says: " . . . handsome officer of the guards, lucky beloved who burns between two fires, but on whom they wasted two presents: the ring with the

protruding diamond the Alba woman gave him and the gold box the Princess gave him." Don Ramón is amused telling about the incidents during which the Princess slips on the ring as Pignatelli is kissing her hand, to make her rival blush and thus expose her, and the Alba woman, furious, broke it off with Pignatelli. For revenge she gave her hairdresser, who was the Princess's too, the gold box that the Princess had given Pignatelli and he to the Duchess. It all ended with Pignatelli's exile to Paris. The author concludes: "The battle began thus; it continues in other ways. The Alba woman outfits her maids in dresses that were imitations of those that arrived from Paris for the Princess . . ." Now we see that Godoy speaks quite correctly of the active and frivolous way that the rivalry between the two women unfolded.

16. The chroniclers' testimony and the story of their respective amorous conquests seem to confirm the high sexual exponent of the protégé and the Duchess, although their portraits make Godoy's words seem a bit exaggerated by today's standards.

17. The ingenuousness with which Godoy, without suspecting it, characterizes himself morally is disturbing. Was he, in his relations with the Queen, anything more than a grateful and stout-hearted gigolo?

18. Her age. She was thirty-eight at that time. Godoy was five years younger.

19. Godoy's resentment toward Fernando VII is so obvious that it takes away from the objectivity of his earnest declarations, but history says that he is not exaggerating, that Spain never had a personality as pernicious and detestable at the head of her government.

20. This does not seem very gentlemanly on Godoy's part toward the Duchess. In her room that night, as he himself confesses later, he did something more than read Fernando's letter . . .

21. For the double wedding of Fernando and Infanta Isabel to the Prince and Princess of Naples, Carlos IV

and María Luisa "threw the house out the window," as they say, from the moment the two Italians landed in Barcelona until their arrival at the palace in Aranjuez in a ship that deserved a place in the *atrezzo* of a Baroque allegory.

22. The truth is that Godoy does not miss the chance to express his opinion of the Prince.

23. A glass practically identical to this, which fits both Goya's and Godoy's description, was displayed in the British Museum in 1979 in its exposition called *The Golden Age of Venetian Glass.*

24. This letter from the Prince to his future mother-in-law has not been preserved in the correspondence of the Queen of Naples. But the baseness of its contents seems to anticipate the famous letter that he sent in October 1807 to the French Emperor.

25. In four lines, Godoy alludes to more nuances of international politics than could be explained in a note, so complex and contradictory was the Spanish diplomatic strategy during Carlos IV's reign. All we need to know is that the letter from Fernando was very disloyal to his parents and, consequently, to his own country's government.

26. The Prince had tutors and teachers, but the years were passing and to the despair of his parents, he did not learn. It is said that he was always quite a simpleton. The words Godoy has him say, nevertheless, in his Memoirs and in this Brief Memoir, attest to a considerable astuteness.

27. There is no other mention of these attacks that perhaps were nothing more than hysterical fits of anger and frustration, which did not develop into the epilepsy that Godoy foists off on him.

28. Wasn't this the same thing that he had done five years before?

29. The Countess of Chinchón's frame of mind was, later on, the cause for several letters from the Queen to

Godoy, full of concern over that stubborn silence she wrapped herself in. On January 3, 1806, María Luisa said: "I wish your wife would have talked to you and had not adopted that complete silence. . . ." And on January 10, 1807: "I deeply regret that your wife was not well and that she was so quiet and therefore injurious to her health; may God keep her well and make her more open and clear-witted. . . ."

MY STORY III

PEPITA showed up unexpectedly at my business office the next afternoon, worried and distressed. What did I know about Cayetana? It seemed she was ill, very ill, she had caught who knows what fevers and the doctors were offering little hope. I left my work half-finished, and we drove the coach at full speed down Arenal Street toward the Buenavista Palace. When we arrived, she had already died. We saw her, lying on her bed, very white under a shroud of white roses that the maids freshened up constantly, lovingly. When we went back to the little parlor, I found myself in front of the dresser. Everything was intact, just the way it looked the night before, including the disorder, and the glass we had drunk from was in its place, but . . . empty! Morose, I had not been able to think about anything but the glass en route from the Royal Palace. And we heard the rumors about the causes of her death in the anteroom. They were so vague and contradictory that each time I felt more intensely that the secret was in the glass. I tried to remember the events of the night before in their exact order, but I could not. I was too confused, struck by Cayetana's death and that premonition that something horrible had happened to her, that those fevers they were talking about were not the cause, that a criminal hand had struck from the shadows. With little remnant of my attention, I listened to what those around me were saying: the Count of Haro, the Count-Duke of Osuna, Cornel. They were all talking about an epidemic and Andalucía. And I kept looking at the empty glass over the Count-Duke's shoulder.

Catalina Barajas, who had aged ten years in one night but who kept herself together and directed the mourners with more efficiency and authority than the men of the house—the distraught Pignatelli and a trail of dazed men who seemed unable to tear themselves away from Cayetana's bed—insisted that we all, men and women, retire to the hall of mirrors while she straightened up the rooms before more people arrived. We obeyed her. But I let a few minutes go by while small groups formed in the hall again. Then, I returned to the little parlor. She was hastily putting away in a chest the things that seemed abandoned on the dresser: some drop earrings, some buckles, a hair comb, an atomizer made of amber. She looked at me with surprise. Given my unexpected return, she stopped her work and leaned toward me, as if waiting for an order, something that could not be done without my say-so. Seeing her surprise, I naturally found it even more difficult to talk, but I managed it. I said, "Last night I was here having a drink with the lady. I drank from that blue glass. I would like . . ." She gave me a long and sad look. "Your Highness surely doesn't think that she drank some poison . . ." she said, softly. A chill ran down my spine. She wrinkled her brow, thoughtfully. "If that is true," she added, "she drank from that glass, too, while I was undressing her . . ." And she stopped herself looking at the glass, astonished. "That's strange," she murmured. "She only drank a few sips. But now it's empty. Who could have . . . ?" She stopped herself again and looked at me. She was a smart woman and was thinking quickly, but she was baffled. "Your Highness hasn't felt ill?" she asked, finally. I shook my head. "Then that couldn't be, right?" Her voice brightened, a glimmer of hope appeared in her eyes. "If you drank from it, too, then she mustn't have been poisoned; it must have been those wretched fevers from Andalucía." She closed the chest and stood waiting for me to leave, to put the final period on that strange conversation. "Except that someone could have slipped in the poison in the interval," I wanted to insist. But I stopped; I did not say it. She stood there, mouth open, as if she had heard my unspoken words pondering, a blank look on her face, head tilted. She suddenly spoke in a voice that was not that of her rank but of her pain as a woman, "And who'd want to harm her like that?" "No one," I said with true feeling. And we stood there in silence. "Pardon me, I'll leave you to work," I said finally. And she answered, "Thank you, Your Highness. Yes, I must get everything in order." She bent her head, picked up the cashmere shawl off the stool and began to fold it. Her question continued to sing in my ear: "And who'd want to harm her like that?" I left.

In the shadow of the hallway, by the light coming in the jalousies in the antechamber, just as I held the door open, I got my answer. I caught a glimpse of the Prince's silhouette, as if magically called up by my fears. There he was, two steps from me. I could not stand to share the narrow hallway with him for more than an instant when we would have to see each other, read each other's thoughts, hear each other's breathing. I stepped back into the parlor. I sensed that he was sneaking into the antechamber, to recover his abominable letter to the Queen of Naples, no doubt. Catalina would be interrupted again. But this time the topic of poison would not be brought up.

I should pause in the story and try to be impartial and not let myself get carried away by my feelings which, after all is said and done, are those of hatred, to explain the theory that I came up with about the death of Cayetana de Alba. No, Catalina, no one wanted to harm your mistress; no one planned to poison her. She was not the intended victim. That victim was I.

Don Fernando hated me, and I was irrevocably his enemy. Jealousy and hatred brought with them the clear sight that allowed him that night to intuit a new humiliation: Cayetana de Alba had gone over to the other side, betrayed him, mocked him with me, together we exposed him to new defeats. As was his custom (and he was an expert at it), the Prince slipped like a rat through the parlors and dark hallways to verify that fact; glued to the door, he heard his fears confirmed and heard his enemy celebrate getting the secret document—which would have further roused his parents' animosity toward him, thus distancing him once more from power. He heard the two traitors toast and imagined them surrendering to the sweetest and most enviable delicacies such as one more toast, mocking their victim even more, whom in turn we can picture yearning, disheartened and impotent, in his hiding place in the hall.[30] Then, the little flask of salts fell to the floor and, in his confusion, hearing a noise and not knowing where it came from, he thought only of escaping. He ran on tiptoe toward the hall of mirrors. Seeing the door to Goya's workshop open, he did not hesitate to hide there. Out of breath and dead with fear (the painter was sketching and had not heard him come in), his eyes like a hunted rat's fell on the table with the spots of paint, on that green powder that, as he had heard a while before, was deadly poison. The temptation was too strong. The traitors had gone into the bedroom; he had heard that. His enemy had promised to toast later with that wine in the priceless glass; he had heard that too . . . The events fell into place without a hitch. Don Fernando grabbed the pot, went back to Cayetana's chambers, became once again the sneaking rat we all know and entered the parlor, sneaked over to the dresser, poured the green powder into the glass, covered his tracks right away, not daring to put the poison back in its place, got rid of it somehow, and joined the party again, where he had not even been missed.

But a half hour later, he saw me come in the parlor and hand him his flask of salts that he probably did not even know he had lost. And what must he have thought right then seeing my ironic smile? That I had found him out, that I had won another battle, had returned to mock him? He did not know that the glass was still in its place, untouched, indiscriminately waiting for its victim. I want to believe that he did not coldly allow Cayetana to be poisoned. That he only understood the truth the next day.

Shaken by pain and crying over the death of their old friend and patron, the people of Madrid proved willing to forget their grievances and dispute over the Juan Hernández gardens. But as often happens in Madrid, affection was soon replaced by curiosity and backbiting; particularly when, at the deceased's expressed wish, the funeral was conducted finally in great secrecy, which did nothing but fan the fires of the gossip concerning her death. Soon all of Madrid was saying that the "Alba woman"—as they called her—had been poisoned, and the guilty parties were being sought everywhere, but above all at the top. No one paid too much attention to the idea that her death was a "punishment from the people," as Goya had said, carried out by the same anonymous hand as the fires, nor did anyone give too much thought to the rumor that the seven heirs, among whom figured her two doctors, could have agreed to cut short their benefactress's days in order to get their inheritance ahead of time. I have said before, in another part of this Memoir, all the rumors were in those days tied to the

Queen and me, and this time our names were not cleared. In the calculations of some evil minds, the old jealousies of the Queen—a rivalry in which I was only one of the pawns—was added to the alliance that the Alba woman had established with the Prince. So, poisoning her was not only a way to clear her from our path, but also a warning to other people who might be tempted to follow in her footsteps and thus bolster Don Fernando's party. With this, naturally, no one had reasons to consider any other suspect; it did not even come out that Cayetana had given a party that evening, that any one of her guests might have had a clear opportunity to poison her food or her drinks. Everyone else believed the rumor that Cayetana died from a long and gradual poisoning, attributed to Cayetana's physical decadence, a slow flux of opium that had finally finished her off. Some people even thought that the Queen and I were caught up in clandestine meetings with strange people versed in the use of poisons and dark ceremonies, black masses, and that Cayetana was probably not our first or our last victim.[31] That was the state of things when I was summoned by Their Majesties to La Granja.

The rumors had reached them, of course. I will not say that they were overly upset by the them, accustomed as they were to being the object of Court slander, but Don Carlos, especially, insisted that the investigation into Cayetana's death be initiated by the Crown itself. Right away, he proclaimed an order that I was to deliver personally to the minister of the interior. That night, while we were playing *crapaud,* the Queen, who knew a lot more about the party than I would have guessed, laid down the deck for a moment and said, "What do you think, Manuel? How did the Duchess die?" I had been expecting that question. "I believe, Majesty, what the doctors believe," I said, "that she died of those Andalusian fevers." "But you were with her that evening. I've heard that even as the night wore on, you two disappeared to her chambers, you must have noticed that she wasn't well . . ." I could not believe it. So great was the Prince's treachery—the desire to wound his mother and to have me be estranged from her—that he had run to tell her that, he had dared to refer to that lapse of time, to his absence when he, in reality, had committed his crime. "With such reliable informants, Majesty, I don't know what I can clarify for you . . ." Doña María Luisa had little patience for this type of indirect conversation and, scrambling the cards on the table—a *crapaud* that of course I had been winning from her—attacked with her brutal frankness, "Come now, Manuel, what were you doing closed up with that woman?" I had the best answer in the inside pocket of my tunic: the copy of the letter from Don Fernando to the Queen of Naples. I laid it on the scattered deck of cards. Now I had no reason to continue keeping the identity of "Il Suggeritore" a secret as I had done up to then. And in passing, clearing up my rendezvous, I discredited her informant once more. Although I would never tell the King and Queen that their firstborn was an assassin, I had more than enough cause to fight him now as if he were the devil himself.

During the few days of the investigation, I received the reports punctually, at the end of the afternoon. No one believed the poison theory. Catalina Barajas did not refer once to her conversation with me, and she limited her comments to "no one would want to harm such a generous woman." No one, apparently, and that was my first relief, testified that the Prince of Asturias had left the party to go upstairs while all the others were listening to the trio. No one saw him enter or leave the deceased's chambers. No one called attention to the Venetian glass, which by then, I now know from Goya, was being lined up among thousands of innocent objects in Cayetana's storeroom. Vexed, the doctors discarded the possibility of error, although neither of their diagnoses coincided; they seemed to reproach each other for certain negligence, both attributing it to the age of his rival, one to youth and the other to old age. The pot of Veronese green was never found (nor did anyone look for it, in truth). It probably disappeared in the rubble from construction on the palace. The flask of salts in its little kid sack fell into obscurity, was recovered and returned to its owner, and neither the owner nor he who found it commented on such an insignificant accident. That small silence was amplified in concentric circles until a total silence covered everything. The people forgot their suspicions with the same frivolousness that they had thought them up. Years later Don Fernando would become King of Spain. With all the reproaches made to him, with all his defects found out, no one ever said he was a murderer.

Notes

30. The choice of the adjective "impotent" does not seem casual. We know that Fernando, although he later remedied the situation, went for nearly a year without consummating his marriage to María Antonia of Naples. This caused concern in both courts, and despair in the Princess herself.

31. It was also rumored, although Godoy does not say so, that he and the Queen had used curare, poison they were both familiar with in some way. María Luisa and her brother Ferdinando, Duke of Parma, in their childhood were actually disciples of Condillac, the French philosopher and founder of the sensualist school. Their interest in him disproves in part the assertion that he had scant intellectual following. Condillac was familiar with South American practices and the studies on curare by La Condamine, who had published in 1751 (the same year

as María Luisa's birth) a short tract on his trip and his discoveries. Godoy was in contact with Humboldt in 1799 (Humboldt was interviewed by Urquijo, then first secretary of state, in Madrid, but he also saw the King, Queen, and Godoy). The naturalist's extremely vast knowledge of the American flora must have included curare. Because of this, theoretically, María Luisa and Godoy were in a position to know everything about the poison and, of course, how to procure it in the Indies. This sort of suspicion clearly did not come from the common people but from cultured people.

EPILOGUE

I DID not go back to see Goya again after our talk that afternoon in Bordeaux. I always kept my last impression of him alive and present: that worn out old man with his beady eyes fixed on the candle that was burning down, like a secret holocaust of his memory, of fidelity, of love. Three years later, at the end of 1828, I learned he had died. A few days before, my daughter had written me from Madrid about the death of Mayte, my wife. I had known for a long time that her health was seriously impaired. This certainly upset my life, for more reasons than just that I had not gone to see her since 1808. In those twenty years of separation, I had not received a single line from her. But now, finally, I was free to marry Pepita, to give my personal life an order and a clear conscience I had never known. The news of Goya's passing away, in the midst of that commotion, did not affect me.

Two months later a friend whom my daughter used as a courier showed up in Rome, bringing me some personal papers. Among them was a letter that simply said: "Give this to Manuel at Mayte's death." I recognized the handwriting: It belonged to my brother-in-law, Luis, who had died in 1823, more than five years before. What could that posthumous message mean? The envelope, sealed with wax, filled me with foreboding. Several days passed before I opened it. I also considered the idea of throwing it in the fire. It did not inspire curiosity in me, but rather fear. Finally, the night before Pepita was to arrive in Pisa, all set to celebrate our wedding with the Pope's permission, I got up my courage and opened it. I do nothing more than transcribe the letter.

A LETTER

My dear Manuel,

I am not a well man. For many months my health has been very bad; I grow worse every day and I feel, with growing and dazzling clarity, that the Lord has decided to call me to his breast. I am still young, not even forty-five, but you know that mine was always a nature plagued by illness. The tensions and anguish of recent times have done nothing to make it any more robust. The doctors try, without success, to deceive me. But I know my days are numbered, and I want to await the end with my soul at peace. That is what brings me to write you. I have borne a heavy burden for twenty years; I want to relieve myself of it now and get ready to die freely, in the best way possible, to receive a Christian death, without any spiritual concerns other than those of my own salvation to keep me on this earth.

I suppose Mayte will not be long in following me. Her health is also frail and broken by years of deep suffering, a suffering the condition of which is difficult to determine. The Mayte of these last three lustrums, a woman whom you have not known or seen—and it is clear to me that she has not written to you either—has done nothing but aggravate those strange, evasive, and incomprehensible elements of her character. Often I can not figure out, even with the great experience the priesthood has given me, whether her pain is moral, spiritual, or simply a cancer of her weakness, a psychic atmosphere that envelops her, traps her, holds her like a prisoner in subtle yet, oh, so diabolical nets. My poor sister. In truth, I do not wish for a long life. And less when I falter. I have been her support—she never has learned how to find the support of divine love for herself—and my absence will certainly do nothing but accentuate her helplessness. Or what if, by chance, I can magnify my moral influence, the radiance of my love for her and the protection I have been and will be able to offer her for a while longer?

But I do not want to, nor should I, allow myself the vanity of talking about myself or of the doubts and anguishes I myself have and will carry with me to my grave. This letter is to talk to you about Mayte. I cannot wander in asides. Probably it is not my place to write this. I certainly do not have the strength to do it. What little God allows me, He is snatching from me day by day, drop by drop. Nevertheless, I have confidence that He, in His mercy, will allow me to finish this letter. Someday you will read it. I have instructed that that be after Mayte's death. With that expressed wish, I leave it in the hands of your daughter, Carlota, so that then and only then she can put it in yours. You will live on, dear Manuel. You have the hearty, robust blood of your peasant background, your valleys of Asturias, not that deliquescent and rarefied liquid that flows through my veins and Mayte's, blood that will cut our passage on this earth short and will take us, perhaps before our souls are really ready, to the portion of the kingdom in the heavens that we deserve.

Mayte will be saved. I pray to the Lord morning and night. I know that she is a basically innocent being whom evil swooped down on like a bird of prey. Evil, for

Mayte, has been nothing more, nothing less than life itself, its duties, its demands, its desires. She was never prepared for it, like a ship that is thrown into the sea, not rigged to resist the pounding waves, a ship that must contend with a storm that its fragile defenses cannot withstand; that she did not succumb to all of it is because of some mysterious instinct for self-preservation—mysterious in a person like her, I mean, with so little instinct, a person so unskilled to navigate the seas. She learned to seek a harbor, a beach where she could be safe. That beach has been my house, my protection, my company, I myself.

Will you allow me, dear brother-in-law, to try to tell you in a few words who Mayte is (who she was, given what has transpired), and what her life has been like, a life that for more than ten years you as husband shared, I daresay, without ever figuring her out or understanding her?

Mayte was raised in an isolated, warm, and overly protected world, the one our parents invented as a domestic refuge in Arenas de San Pedro, to which in a certain way their marriage and their exclusion from the Crown, the Court, and the prerogatives of the royal family condemned them. We were royalty, but we could not call ourselves that; we were a good and normal bourgeois family, but we considered ourselves royalty. We were on the fringe of two worlds, segregated from the Court and unable to integrate ourselves into an unfamiliar and simpler society, where tradition and privilege carried less weight. We were alone. An island. And on that island Mayte and I were born. She grew up sweet and vulnerable as she was from the cradle, always feeling the protection of her older brother, who, three years older, adopted her from the first. Even the later arrival of another sister did not change things for that unique little pair that went through childhood in a nearly mystical union, created from unconditional love, from unquestioned support, from secret games. An island inside another island. I protected her from her physical weakness, her fears, and from all the rest—strangers and adults. She let me be her knight errant and in turn made me feel stronger and more intrepid than I really was, if only in comparison to her helplessness. We were happy. We would have gone on that way if life had not assaulted us with its demands. I am referring to the outside world, the world that forced us to abandon the pleasures of our garden, populated by small insects and small mysteries, butterflies and dreams, and the sanctuary of our winter games, in the rooms under the eaves inhabited by wooden soldiers, toy swords, fake beards, offspring of our dolls, and the ghostly inventions of our magic lantern.

Then, the time came to leave all that behind, to enter into adult life. Fearing that separation, I took a step to safeguard myself that perhaps was cowardly and a betrayal to Mayte: I chose religion. That career, to my adolescent eyes, did not take me as far from my magic circle as arms or diplomacy—in a word, the world—would have. She went on growing, at great pains, against her will, with no hope, hanging on to my progress in piety or theology, more than on her own progress as a budding woman, growth that was bringing to her natural grace, custom, fashions, and the prospect of a future marriage. In the end, we two still dreamed of returning to our garden. In fact, when my ecclesiastical studies permitted it, we did just that: We returned to our butterfly collection, which she added to in my absence to surprise me, or we would sit down again, fingers interlaced, before our magic lantern to make images, pious ones now, the ones that touched us the most, such as flights to Egypt, Annunciations, angels rising from Tobias's hands.

As you can see by now, I cannot talk of Mayte without talking about myself. It's useless to fight it. Perhaps that is what makes this letter so important to me; perhaps that explains why I would want to write to someone about this before I die, a desire beyond merely easing my own conscience. If I have chosen you as a depository of all this, perhaps it is because you are the third person in this story, Manuel. The one who, without meaning to, represented the invasion by Life, with all its cruelty, its dominion, its blindness in a world as closed, as complete, as vulnerable as ours. Imagine an empty egg, at the same time incomparably unassailable and incomparably fragile.

Your marriage to Mayte was decided upon behind our backs; I would say behind our own parents' backs; they were consulted by our cousin, the King, but in terms that left little margin for discussion or protest. Nothing is more despotic than a sovereign favor. In my father's defense, I should say that he, as much as he loved my mother, never stopped feeling guilty for his morganatic union and for having made his children what he affectionately but sadly called "my little pariahs." In some way, the offer from Don Carlos IV gave him, I believe, the chance to repair that injustice at least to Mayte, who now would be able to have a title, as he did, to call herself Countess of Chinchón and, through her marriage to you, would accede to the highest circles of Court life. It all happened, you will remember, with extraordinary speed. As for myself, I was busy with my own honors and vanities—His Holiness had just bestowed on me the cardinal's hat—and so I did not get involved in giving the serious thought required in such a matter—the fact that my sister was being sacrificed on the altars of disputable reasons of state. And do not be annoyed if I speak of sacrifices, dear Manuel: It is not to discredit or tarnish your character that I say that, because I believe that you were also a victim of that brutal custom.

You and Mayte should never have married one another; you were not made for one another. What was gained in that union turned out to be, in the end, vastly insignificant compared with what had been hoped for and imagined by the authors of that marriage. But to tell the truth, Mayte herself did not rebel for one minute against the destiny that was procured so neglectfully for her by the monarchs with their idea, by my parents with their consent, and even by you with your acceptance. Also she submitted, being barely sixteen, not mentally, morally, or even physically mature. And she did it, if not happily, at least with the soft, submissive disposition with which she always obeyed our parents. Who knows? She may have also fooled herself more than a little with the change of status and honors awaiting her. In those weeks, I remember we two had our portraits done by Maestro Goya, the good Francisco, I in my flame-red cardinal's robes; she, I would say, disguised as the woman of the world that she would begin to be. We both were vain about our respective, parallel, and shining destinies. But there is something that always has surprised me when I look at those two portraits. There is such a deep insecurity in our bearing and expression, such absence of aplomb and confidence, and such resplendence of uncertainty in our eyes, which reveal to me an unconfessed truth: We were not as deceived by the honors as we wanted to believe or make everyone think. We are two frightened children looking out at the world: I, at the height of my ecclesiastical fortunes, she, at the height of her fortunes as a woman of the Court. God willed that I should bear mine better. Up to a certain point. The disgrace that swooped down on my beloved sister was also my Calvary. Thus, through a decision made by everyone else and by our frivolous acquiescence, we left paradise forever.

As a priest, I know that it is very difficult to completely penetrate the intimate life of a married couple. Although, from the first, Mayte sought a refuge in me for her failed marriage, she never was explicit in defining the reasons for that failure. I always thought that her first experiences with the obligations of marriage must have been extremely cruel and violent for her. She was not prepared for that, nor can I imagine her even slightly guided by instinct or by diligent women friends down the sinuous adolescent roads of sensuality. The first visit I made to your house after the marriage, I knew it. Something had broken in Mayte—and it was not physical. Her eyes had become apprehensive, very sad; her walk, unsteady or ungainly, wavering; her voice, timid and childish, lusterless, lifeless. Something was broken, mutilated, stunted; instead of flowering into a woman, Mayte stopped growing, turned in on herself, disappeared. As if her first contact with Life had terrorized her once and for all. I don't know, dear Manuel, what your carnal relationship really was with her; at times, I have even thought that what horrified her was having discovered her own wild passion, a carnality too bestial that must have been awakened in her. Because of that she felt ashamed, humiliated, condemned. I don't know. In any case, with you the dominations had erupted in her life: the world, the devil, the flesh. You were not free to give her the love that can ransom a person from that terror, true? She had no other way out except to flee, flee inside herself, toward that inner sea of silence that, you will recall, before you left Spain, had overwhelmed her and had given us chills.

First it was that revulsion, that fear; afterward came maternity, and once again nature, with its implacable demands, was a trial that was too hard for her. It was a difficult and accidental pregnancy, a birth that almost cost her her life, a revealing indifference toward her newborn daughter. She was not the daughter of love but, let me repeat, of sacrifice. Or perhaps of shame, the result of an appetite that could not be reconciled by the little girl from Arenas, what Mayte had most wanted to go on being for my sake. Poor Carlota, you know, has grown up without a mother, which explains her demanding, tyrannical, and insatiable nature. Yet now she is the one who must watch over Mayte when I am not there to do it, watch over the mother who never served that role or wanted her as such. Carlota's birth was the second circle of hell that Mayte began to descend to as a result of her marriage to you. Also the portrait Francisco did of her during her pregnancy (commissioned by me, since I still did not admit the magnitude of the disaster) summarizes that stupor and panic she was living and was trying to forget as she pretended to return with me to our childhood games. But we were no longer in Arenas de San Pedro. I was already twenty-three and archbishop of Toledo; she was twenty and was about to give her first offspring to the Prince of Peace. After that, the tragedy incubated. The foreboding of a destroyed and hopeless life! I myself, even though I tried to help her in the faith and in my pastoral activities, could not manage to drive from my mind the hopeless melancholy in Mayte's eyes.

Later, she told me much more, reliving in outbursts and anguish the horror of those hours. At the peak of her agony in childbirth, she saw you as the devil who had inflicted those torments on her. Yes, Manuel, in her imagination you changed nature and hierarchy: You were Lucifer himself. And from that moment, darkly, from the formless body of her irrational hatred, there began to grow, deformed but clear, fantasized but corporeal, a monster: the desire for revenge. It was the only answer she saw; she was wounded, she felt destroyed, she wanted to give in; she would drink that suffering down to the last drop, as her predestined chalice, but she would have her revenge. She did not know how or when. She only knew her victim. She began to have hallucinations, to dwell on your death and your own torment. But all the finales—the battlefield, a wild horse, a fever—seemed too tame to her. She dreamed of you quartered, strangled, burned. And even that was little payment for her vengeance. She overlooked the fact that she lacked the liberating element: She and no one else must carry out that revenge. That was the only way she would establish order, justice, harmony in this world. Then she could hunt butterflies with me again and impale them in our glass case in Arenas. All this I learned much later, too late. If it had been otherwise, I would have warned you, and perhaps I would have done some good. At least you two would have separated eight years before and not waited for your fall and your exile, and the worst would have been avoided. Because the worst came to be. And that is the heart of this letter.

Do you remember the last party Cayetana de Alba gave on the very night of her death? You and I attended, and I imagine Cayetana's sudden and surprising demise has etched that particular party in our memory, but I am going to talk to you about the party as Mayte lived it, as she finally described it to me several years later. I will try not to go into unnecessary details. Mayte, you will remember, arrived at the Buenavista Palace in my company, believing you to be in La Granja. We had no more arrived when we saw you among the guests and Pepita among them also. That was the first blow for Mayte. She said she was not jealous of Pepita and did not wish her ill. What's more, she sympathized with her; she considered her another victim of your malignant mind. But seeing you both there, she interpreted it as a trap that had been set for her (with everyone in on it—you, Cayetana, Pepita), an affront, a public slap in the face, a joke. By that time, Mayte had become obsessed with the idea of being the permanent object of everyone's joke, yours especially, that you directed the game to that end. She never attributed your blunders, tactlessness, misunderstanding to anything but a pure and simple desire to offend her personally, to ridicule her, to solicit the ironic complicity of others in your perverse plan. It was a bad beginning for that party. From that point on, Mayte continued to lack composure, continued to be susceptible, thinking everyone's looks ranged from sarcasm to pity, fearing the night would bring her even worse moments. When she saw you chatting with Cayetana off in a corner, she interpreted that as a provocation too. (She knew that you were seeing her secretly; she was having you followed.) She heard whispers and laughter and once again felt she was the butt of a joke. To her your wickedness had no limits; she could imagine you discussing some intimacy or her ineptness as mother or as homemaker. Curiously, her fantasy lived side by side with enough sense of reality so she could go on developing it without awakening suspicions or alarm in anyone. The least detail was fuel to her. Since she confided in no one and confronted no one with her conjectures, they grew stronger in her spirit to the point of being the rigid iron bars that imprisoned her and behind which she secretly and uselessly struggled in her humiliation.

Later, during dinner, Cayetana joked about the attempted fires at Buenavista and dealt out guilt to those present. In her daring game, Cayetana named the Queen herself, you, the Osuna woman, even the common people as possible bearers of the treacherous torches. Mayte tried to speak up, propose herself as a possible incendiary hand, and managed to say in her little, flat voice, "Your dresses are just so elegant, Cayetana. Didn't anyone tell you they saw me the other afternoon, driving through the Prado in my carriage, holding a lighted torch?" As always when she tried to be ironic, she took too long to get to the point, she was not direct, she lost everyone's attention. In a word, she had tried to make a joke. No one heard her. Her words fell into a void. Cayetana answered her with a passing comment that showed she was not paying attention. And Mayte felt, once again, rejected, diminished. She did not count at that table; she was no one, not even numbered among possible enemies. She was on the verge of leaving her seat. The fact that not even her dining partners at the table noticed her state did nothing but confirm her fears: She did not exist, or if she did, it was only to be scorned.

Then came the walk through the palace, the stop in Francisco's workshop, Cayetana's performance regarding the poisonous paints. During the walk, Mayte was thinking about nothing but her delayed vengeance, just out of reach, and was surrendering to her fantasy of ways you could actually die: She saw you plunging headlong down the enormous marble staircase, lying at the bottom, a crumpled rag doll. She had to grab the banister to keep from fainting. The fire of those very torches would come together in a single pyre and crackle as it burned your demons, expelling them in one great holocaust. The oil from the torches made her so nauseous that she had to cover her nose and breathe in the perfume on her handkerchief. Cayetana's discourse on the poison created an image that was at the same time an echo of those words and also a more concrete vision: you, writhing on the ground, agonizing with no remedy or help, wailing with your punishment, with everyone else transformed into indifferent, disdainful, or condemning statues. It was easy, Cayetana said. You only had to sniff, to taste, to touch to the end of your tongue that little emerald green powder. She would just have to mix it in your snuff, sprinkle it on lettuce, dump it in the water you drank at night, Mayte thought. The images filled her with ecstasy; for a moment—finally!—she had seen you dead and she had her reward. God had heard her, she could live peacefully the rest of her days, forgetting you. She fainted.

When she came to, I was by her side, no one was talking about poisons, she looked at you and saw just some man, not the devil. That only happened to her in those rare moments. She was awakened to reality for a moment. But it did not last long. After a while, we left there, once she seemed to regain her strength. At the doorway to the hall of mirrors, we ran into Francisco, who was returning. Just then, the devil confronted her with another jealous moment. She turned her gaze away by chance and in the mirrors saw you and Cayetana, leaving in the half-dark of the back hall. You two were embracing, she thought she saw you kissing, you were whispering like conspirators or lovers, you slipped inside the room and cautiously closed the door behind you. Cayetana's eyes arrogantly met hers. Once again, the scorn. She clutched my arm to avoid another fainting spell, and we left. The minute of reality had passed.

When Cayetana's chaplain offered to show us the chapel and I accepted, she gave an excuse: She preferred to rest there, waiting for the musicians. I left her then, seated among the other guests, and went with the chaplain. Once more, I did not divine the hurricane of jealousy and hate that were filling that soft and shining little head. She did not wait long. By her side was Fernando. We had never been his friends, because his cruelty and duplicity had forced a wedge between us since childhood. But a close bond of kinship united us, and she could, in some ways, confide in him. She told him that she was resting for a minute, since she feared becoming ill again and interrupting the musicians. Fernando offered her his flask of salts again. She accepted, took them, and left right away. The vestibule was empty, the stairway, too, lighted by just a few torches. She went quickly upstairs, crossed galleries and salons, saw even her terror reflected and multiplied in crystals and mirrors, but she went on, dazzled, drawn like a magnet toward Cayetana's room. She passed by Francisco's workshop. The door was open; Francisco was drawing, his back turned to the salon. She did not stop. She went on down the pitch dark back hallway, groped along the walls until she found the door that she had seen close behind you two, pressed herself to it, and listened.

At first she did not understand what you were talking about—a letter, Naples, things she knew nothing about. But suddenly you began to talk about wine, a glass, a toast. There were silences, and she could imagine what was going on between you two, and her desperation redoubled. If she heard you laughing, you were still laughing about her. Her hatred toward you was growing, and her need to destroy you, when something happened, a thud, a muffled noise at her feet (she did not know the cause), and a sudden silence in the room and the cold sweat and fear of being discovered. She fled. The hall of mirrors seemed interminable. She would not have managed to cross it and disappear in time, if one of you was following her. She noticed that the door to Goya's workshop was open, and she slipped through it. Francisco still had his back turned; he had not noticed her come in. She heard footsteps at the far end of the hallway. She thought it was you. She trembled. But when you did not lean inside the workshop, she was saved and . . . she had fooled you! The footsteps went away, the door closed lightly but sharply in the funereal silence. She stayed there, unnoticed by Goya, exalted, recovering her breath but still burning with vindictive fury, a small, trembling, helpless nemesis with her pale rose dress and her little bird face lost in that scary solitude. She had seen on the table, just in her reach, the flask of green paint that half an hour before had been what Francisco and Cayetana had been fighting about. The words were still ringing in her ear, along with the pounding of her recent fainting spell. Lethal poison! The devil had played his cards well.

She went back out the door to the hallway, with the poison in her hands, like a chalice. She listened. There was not a sound. You were probably together in the bedroom. But you had promised to drink the wine later in that beautiful glass, yes, you had promised. She did not have to do anything but go in and put a little of the powder in the glass she saw on the dresser. Too preoccupied in the bedroom, you would not hear her. She went in, with the cautious and airy step she had learned chasing butterflies. The glass, she saw it and identified it right away. A blue and gold butterfly! She poured a little poison in the wine. She did not hear anything. There is the same magical silence around the hunter of butterflies, too. The powder floated on top of the wine. She stirred it with the silver and diamond cross that hung around her neck, the cross I had given her as a wedding present. She dried the cross on the fringe of a shawl on the floor next to the dresser. She went out, stealthily, the way she had come in. She had caught her butterfly. What ecstasy!

I picture her, machinelike, crossing the hall of mirrors, that now multiplied to infinity her secret triumph. In the gallery she opened one of the windows, the fresh air of the Madrid night pulled her from her trance: She understood that she ought to get rid of the poison, and she threw it into the patio. She heard it make a dull clatter. She went downstairs. She took her place again among the guests. The trio was beginning its program. She saw Fernando and remembered the flask of salts. She did not have it; she could not return it to him. Where had she lost it? He was going to ask for it back soon; it was a beauty. Once again the anguish. Applause rewarded the musicians. The guests were talking among themselves. Fernando, for the moment, forgot to ask her for the flask. She felt the impulse to ask me for help. But I had gone to visit the chapel, and she did not feel up to facing the dark palace again, looking for me, although she would have liked to have gone into the oratory, pray, beg for help, support, guidance. She clutched the crucifix in her right fist and prayed there, alone, with no one realizing it, no one paying attention to her. That was an advantage of the confusion at the party. Or more likely, they saw her there, isolated from everyone, fist at her breast, eyes lowered, and supposed that she still had not recovered completely from her fainting spell. The music began again. She sighed, relieved. That gave her time. Time for everything. Time to pray. Time for me to return and take her hands, restoring the energies she had lost. Time for you, there above, as you were leaving the bedroom, to pick up the glass and drink. She saw you do it. Go barefoot and half-naked to the dresser, pick up the glass, raise it in a toast and drink deeply from it . . . The glass would shatter on the floor. She heard a long moan of pain. It was only the transverse flute singing its dramatic saraband. And Cayetana had already returned, her eyes very bright, her walk nonchalant, passing by Mayte without seeing her, sidling up close to the musicians, to sit on the floor, half-lying on a cushion, from there to listen to the end of the score. What had happened? Had you returned alone upstairs and were you about to pick up the glass and drink, or had Cayetana left you writhing in pain on the divan in her dressing room? And yet you had not cried out. A cry of agony must, by force, cross the salons and galleries, come down the stairway, and search out the ear of the one waiting for it as the only prize possible for such fear. But the cry did not come. In its place, she heard men's voices, animated, full, coming from the vestibule, and when she turned, it was you and I, walking in with the chaplain. The guests were applauding, getting to their feet and surrounding the musicians. From under her half-closed eyelids, she saw you walk over to Fernando and hand back the flask of salts.

It seemed to her that once again you were laughing, that Cayetana, still sitting on the floor, was laughing inside, too. Once again they were mocking her, making fun of her. She had uselessly put poison in the glass. You were smarter. You had not drunk from it. She could not hold back; she let a moan slip out. I went to help her, as always, but you were closer, and you got to her before me. You offered to take her home, and I could not keep you from it. She, of course, never opposed. Her submission was also a vengeance. I know that you two rode home in silence. She hoped the whole way home that you would say something about the poison. She would have preferred that. It was worse that you said nothing, that you ignored her. For once, she had been able to confront you, to attack you, to return to you in the same coin of cruelty the thousand deaths that you had caused her. She hated you more than ever, because you had made her suffer.

The next day she found out about Cayetana's death. And she understood what had happened. It was something she had never considered for a single moment. The poison was meant for you. Why was God playing that terrible joke on her? She could not go to the funeral. She fell into a tremendous nervous prostration (which in truth did not surprise anyone, so deplorable was her health in those days) and feared she would rave and incriminate herself. Her act of justice had been turned into a crime by the mysterious design of Providence.

I do not need to tell you that I learned none of this in the sanctity of confession. It was two years later that, all of a sudden, she told it all to me. One summer day, she showed up in my archbishopric in Toledo, transparent, worn thin by anguish. She told me that she needed a rest from her little girl and from household chores, that she was coming to stay one, two, three weeks, as long as I would have her. I guessed that she needed something more than my company, but I refrained from saying anything to her. I hoped that she would come out with it herself. For several days, she wandered, aimlessly, around Toledo, losing herself in the cloisters, crossing over bridges, baking in the sun, or slipping like a shadow around the archbishopric, headed nowhere in particular, elusive, quiet, vague, and tenuous, like one of those butterflies we used to hunt when we were children. But I did not set out to hunt her down. I was waiting for her to alight, to come to me. I knew that eventually she would. One day, as we were resting from the dog days under an old olive tree, she collapsed ever so slowly at my side, like a figure in a dream and, holding my hand in my lap, she began to talk very slowly, as if she were just going on with a story that she had been telling forever and that somehow did not exist at any point in time. She told me everything. It was very strange. She was not repentant. She did not feel guilty or responsible. You were still to blame for everything. For her suffering, for her sleepless nights, and yes, for her actions that night, too. But she could not go on living alone with her secret. She knew that I could help her bear it, just like when we were children and we could not bear our secrets anymore. We would retreat to the shadows of an elm or the darkest corner of the attic, with our toys, to tell each other, under oath, something as innocent as having asked the Three Wise Men for a new net, having broken the porcelain doll's finger in a careless moment, or having written a play for our father's saint's day. This is the way she talked to me, telling a secret, as if sharing it with me were the only way to make what she was telling me seem important, and as if what she was telling me were trivial. Cayetana's death by poison was no more important than those broken doll's fingers. I knew at that point that she was mad.

That story seemed to start nowhere but at the beginning of those days, in her childhood in Arenas de San

Pedro, and lasting all those days and nights in Toledo, it seemed not to have any end either, except in that youth gathered together from that death that was ours, too. I was twenty-seven then; she was no more than twenty-five. But it seemed there was nothing left to us for the rest of our days, but for one to tell the story and the other to listen, one to be upset and one to calm the other, one to feel hopeless and the other to console, her at my feet, her little, sweaty hand in my trembling one, both hands in my sweaty, sterile lap forever. She stayed for several months. I do not remember how many. Her tale was like one unending wake, where I poured all my devotions. I was working a lot then on my pastoral duties. But that time did not count, it seemed in vain, it was only a respite from true time, the time spent on the story with no beginning and no end.

When you left Spain, four years later, she gathered her household goods together, without a single word between her and me, and came to live with me once and for all. This time, she brought the little girl, who was now a big girl and who brightened the hours with her charms. But Mayte was always lying in wait at night, expecting the nursemaids to take care of Carlota, waiting to prop herself up against my knees and tell me stories. It was curious. She did not want to know a thing about you; she did not answer your letters; she brushed away, disgusted, the letters you wrote me; she changed the subject abruptly and harshly if anyone asked about you. Then, in the late night silence, you were her only topic, and she was surrounded ad infinitum by memories of your life together. It is true, all these memories seemed to congeal on a certain July 22, as if the devil had been exorcised that night with the ordered, linked, and fatal series of images, objectively exhibited and polished to exhaustion: the kiss in the mirror, the poison on Goya's table, the glass on the dresser, the silver cross stirring the wine . . . And the other vision, the one she imagined: Cayetana drinking the poison by mistake after the party.

Time passed. I had political responsibilities that kept me far away from Toledo and from her, even though I could not get her out of my thoughts. I was in Cádiz with the Court, in Madrid keeping busy with the Regency, in Valencia receiving Fernando, whom people came to call "El Deseado." When I returned in 1814, banished by the King to Toledo, I found her very changed. She had begun to take refuge in her devotions and sweets. She had turned into a stout, placid woman with a very childish, very simple look on her face, who only talked about praying and eating, about God and nougats, not distinguishing one thing from the other very much. My banishment lasted six years and was very sad, not so much because of seeing myself separated from politics by the sovereign's decision—and distrust—rather because of my melancholy contemplation of that transformed Mayte, who no longer lay in wait at night for the moment when she could be alone with me. Now she was the Mayte who closed herself up to eat candy that the doctor vainly tried to forbid. She almost never spoke of the past anymore. When she did, they were cold, barren, impersonal references, like someone who is resigned to giving two or three essential points of a topic too well-known to warrant her full attention or what was left of her emotions. All this, I suppose is the relative salvation that madness knows how to find down torturous and indirect roads. One way to avoid things and survive. One Our Father, ten marzipans, a Gloria. God will find a way to forgive me for this irreverence, but I want to give you the version closest to the truth.

Three years ago, in 1820, when the liberals came back to power and forced Fernando to reinstate the Constitution, I returned to politics, as you know, as president of the Provincial Council. Once again, I put many miles between Mayte and me. She has stayed in Toledo, but her life took on a third obsession when Carlota arrived, along with her Italian husband and the children who've kept on coming; she has now added her grandchildren to her piety and to her gluttony. That late birth of maternal feelings is amazing in a woman who could feel absolutely nothing for her own daughter. There is nothing left now of that little girl from Arenas, of the young girl who was waiting for me when my studies in theology ended, of that pale, trembling woman who turned up in Toledo twenty years ago. However, I know that hers has been a life filled with suffering, an agony masked by tranquility. She is too fat; the doctors have given up hope of curing her obesity, and she does not cooperate with them in any way except to agree that she is sick. They don't expect her to live for many more years.

She will outlive me after all this. I am spent now, Manuel. Add to my always bad health the worries I have had, living in this country these fifteen years of invasions, brothers fighting brothers, hopes truncated again and again, and failures, failures, failures. Add to that, Mayte's pain that is my own, that has not left me for a minute the whole time. Having lost her—first in your hands, then in the hands of this mental illness—has been a privation of which I have never learned to console myself, even to the point that I still remember nostalgically those years in Toledo when I looked forward to seeing her fall on her knees at my feet, take my hand, lean her head on my purple lap, and tell me the story that had no beginning and no end, of her tragedy. A tragedy that was—is—one with my own.

Have you ever seen one of Francisco's Caprichos he called *Volaverunt?* A woman is flying through the air, with a butterfly on her forehead, like a great, shining star, a tangle of monsters at her feet. Each time I see it I think of Mayte's soul, which always hoped to fly on the tenuous fluttering of the butterflies from her childhood, on the soft, warm, murmuring mystery of our shared adolescence. She could no more take off from the ground than she could conjure from her path those monsters: the world, the devil, the flesh, all that you summoned to her life without meaning to.

Again I tell you: This is not an accusation, Manuel. But your ignorance of Mayte, her suffering, the cross she had to bear pains me like a flame. I can not keep from writing you. And now I have done it. It has cost me too much of my strength. I have probably shortened my life even more. I should go into seclusion. I pray to the Lord that He not delay in taking me to Him. I hope He comes this very night. I will await Him along with Mayte: not the Mayte of today, but the one I remember; not the one of the monsters, but the one of the butterflies.

God be with you, Manuel. Your brother-in-law (who would have wished never to have been so)

Luis

I received this letter twenty years ago. Shortly after that, I began to adjust to it. Slowly and painstakingly, I have canceled out my own story about the night of July 22, 1802. After all is said and done, my entire error is born of sleight of hand: Without my knowing it, the flask of salts passed from the Prince's hands to Mayte's and that lone, insignificant detail invalidates what was my deep conviction for nearly thirty years; the Prince is washed clean of blame; it snatches from me that trump card I could have played—but never did—in the face of judgment over the centuries. It is true that Luis's letter revealed to me an ignorance more terrible than who did or did not have the flask of salts: my ignorance of Mayte, of what lurked at the bottom of her silences. Where do the crimes in this diabolical story begin?

In one of my moves, I mislaid the drawing by Goya, the one of the maja and the glass of poison. I have never seen the print of it, which both he and Luis told me about: *Volaverunt.* Would I have found yet another meaning in it? I have forgotten my Latin. I don't even know what that word means: Volaverunt . . .

Paris, 1848

A NOTE FROM THE AUTHOR

Years ago, I was asked to collaborate on a biography of Goya for television. Although the project was aborted in its early stages, I had done a considerable amount of research on the subject and remained captivated by a few images: Goya in his studio, making up the Duchess of Alba; the Duchess setting fire to her palace in the middle of a party; Godoy, decrepit, old, and forgotten, in exile in Paris. Of these ghosts, which would not leave me in peace, *The Last Portrait of the Duchess of Alba* was born.

There will always be a certain amount of mystery surrounding events in the Spain Goya knew—a Spain of scandal, intrigue, and, ultimately, decline—but there is much in the preceding pages I know to be true. Almost all of the characters, those of the Court, the members of Cayetana's household, the bullfighters, actors, and statesmen, did exist. Their likenesses can be seen in Goya's paintings, sketches, and prints. The Duchess had a celebrated affair with the artist, as well as intimate associations with other prominent men of the time, including opponents of the Crown. A woman of extraordinary beauty, she was clearly at the center of Madrid society and may very well have indulged in the "powder of the Andes," which was the obsession of the day. Goya immortalized her in many famous works. *The Naked Maja,* in particular, was later found in the inventory of Godoy's possessions. She also appears in the capricho called *Volaverunt,* now in the Prado. It shows a maja born aloft by a butterfly at her head, while grotesque monsters gather at her feet. It was made a few years before the Duchess's death on July 23, 1802. Of course, the actual cause of her death remains unknown.

Antonio Larreta
Madrid, 1987

ABOUT THE MAKING OF THIS BOOK

The text of *The Last Portrait of the Duchess of Alba* was set in Janson by ComCom, a division of The Haddon Craftsmen, of Allentown, Pennsylvania. The book was printed and bound by Maple-Vail Book Manufacturing Group of Binghamton, New York. The typography and binding were designed by Tom Suzuki of Falls Church, Virginia.